D1017387

Geronimo Stilton

OUT OF TIME

THE EIGHTH JOURNEY THROUGH TIME

Scholastic Inc.

Library of Congress Cataloging-in-Publication Data available

ISBN 978-1-338-68712-5

Text by Geronimo Stilton
Original title *Viaggio nel tempo-8*
Art director: Iacopo Bruno
Cover by Silvia Bigolin, Christian Aliprandi, and Emilio Ignozza/ theWorldofDOT
Illustrations by Ivan Bigarella, Federico Brusco, Andrea Denegri, Alessandro Muscillo, Carla Debernardi, and Christian Aliprandi
Graphics by Marta Lorini

Special thanks to Julia Heim
Translated by Rebecca Herrick
Interior design by Kay Petronio

10 9 8 7 6 5 4 3 2 1   21 22 23 24 25

Printed in China   62

First edition, January 2021

Geronimo Stilton

OUT OF TIME

THE EIGHTH JOURNEY THROUGH TIME

VOYAGERS ON THE EIGHTH JOURNEY THROUGH TIME

Geronimo Stilton

My name is Stilton, Geronimo Stilton. I am the editor-in-chief of *The Rodent's Gazette*.

Thea Stilton

My sister, Thea, is athletic and brave! She's also a special correspondent for *The Rodent's Gazette*.

TRAP

My cousin Trap is a terrible prankster sometimes! His favorite hobby is playing jokes on me ... but he's family, and I love him!

Benjamin

Benjamin is my favorite little nephew. He's a sweet and caring ratlet, and he makes me so proud!

Bluster Squeak

This mouse was my history teacher in high school, and he is also a skilled inventor and a friend of Paws von Volt, Beaker Poirat, and Cyril B. Sandsnout.

Beaker Poirat

He is a marvemouse scientist, with a phenomenal brain! He is the one who invented the Bananacraft, the time machine we use in this adventure.

Cyril B. Sandsnout

Professor Sandsnout is the director of the Archaeology Mouseum of New Mouse City, and is also a great friend of mine. He travels the world looking for mysterious papyrus scrolls and archaeological relics.

Trappy

This is my lively niece Trappy! She is a mischievous rascal who is identical to Trap in every way — including pulling pranks on me!

Creepella von Cacklefur

Creepella is an enchanting journalist from Mysterious Valley. She also has a huge crush on me and keeps saying she wants to marry me . . . but I'm not interested!

AREN'T YOU IN THE MOUSITI ISLANDS?!

I should've known that day would be **TERRIBLE**. Not just **TERRIBLE** — **REALLY, MOUSERIFICALLY TERRIBLE**!

Does that ever happen to you? When, first thing in the **morning**, you realize that everything that can go wrong that day *will* go wrong?

Ouch, ouch, ouchie!

That morning, I woke up early and — squeak! I'm sorry, I haven't introduced myself! My name is Stilton, *Geronimo Stilton*, and I run *The Rodent's Gazette*, the most famous newspaper on Mouse Island.

As I was saying: as usual, I had gotten up and gone to work. At the office, my assistant, **Mousella**, greeted me by saying, "Good morning, Mr. Stilton! Why are you so PALE? Hurry — they are all waiting for you in the conference room, with Mr. Shortpaws!"

"Huh? GRANDFATHER WILLIAM?" I muttered as I climbed the stairs. "He doesn't work here anymore!" He retired from *The Rodent's Gazette* many years ago. Last I heard, he was on vacation in the MOUSITI ISLANDS!

I opened the door to the conference room and couldn't believe my eyes. It was really him: my grandfather, the one, the only . . . **William Shortpaws**!

"G-G-Grandfather!" I stammered. "What are you doing here? Aren't you in the Mousiti Islands?"

Suddenly, I realized my grandfather wasn't there in the fur and whiskers — he was a HOLOGRAM!

"You call *this* an early start?!" Grandfather thundered. "Is this how you run *my* newspaper?!"

I tried to respond. "Er, well, you entrusted it to me many years ago, and —"

"Silence!" he roared, making me JUMP in fright — and hit my head on the side of the door. Ouch, ouch, ouchie!

Grandfather continued his tirade. "I knew that I shouldn't have retired. *The Rodent's Gazette* is still in need of mice like me! Now sit down, and let's begin the MEETING."

I took a seat at the table, my whiskers trembling.

Thea leaned toward me and whispered, "Did you really need to make Grandfather angry? You know how he is!"

"I didn't do it on purpose!" I squeaked. "Who knew he would be here?! I mean, he's not *here*, he's *there*, in the Mousiti Islands, but he's also here while he's there, and . . . how did he even manage to use this crazy new technology?!"

"Cool, isn't it?" Thea said. "It's all thanks to Beaker Poirat!"

"Beaker Poirat?"

"Silence!" Grandfather Shortpaws roared again, making me jump in fright — and BITE my tongue. Ouch, ouch, ouchie!

Ouch, ouch, ouchie!

Grandfather turned his fiery

BEAKER POIRAT

FIRST NAME: Beaker

LAST NAME: Poirat

PROFESSION: Scientist/inventor

EDUCATION: He has thirteen degrees in the following subjects: Reactive Pistachio Science, Pistachius Accelerator Science, Green Neuronic Science, Science of the Pistachiacious Shell, Techniques of Energetic Pistachio Extrapolation, Prototonic Pistachions, the Nutritive Theory of Dried Fruit, the Science of the Pistachiosphere Improbability, Pistachio Phenomenology, Pistachiatic Enigmas, Communicative Techniques of Pistachio Shells, the Study of Effects of Pistachio Indigestion on the Inventive Process, and the Origins of Pistachios.

DISTINGUISHING TRAITS: If you couldn't already tell, he adores pistachios.

ILLUSTRIOUS RELATIVES: His cousin Hercule Poirat is the most famouse detective in New Mouse City.

FRIENDS: Professor Paws von Volt, Professor Bluster Squeak, Professor Cyril B. Sandsnout

gaze toward me. "Still a lazyfur, I see! You never change!"

Then he turned to Thea and said affectionately, "Thea, my dear! You are always prompt and organized. Could you kindly go over the AGENDA?"

"Of course, Grandfather!" Thea said. "We must:

1 Approve the cover for Geronimo's latest novel.

2 Review drawing samples from illustrators.

3 Choose a title for our new series of joke books and puzzle books.

4 Decide on the number of pages in the next *Journey Through Time* book."

Grandfather William clapped his paws, nodding in satisfaction. "Bravo! Well done, my favorite grandchild!"

Then he turned toward me, pointing. "Do you see how it's done, Geronimo?!"

That gave me such a fright, I jumped up and

Ouch, ouch, ouchie!

BANGED my knee on the table. Ouch, ouch, ouchie!

Why, why, why does everything always happen to me?

Grandfather continued relentlessly. "You should learn from your sister, Geronimo. She is really a true Stilton! Now get to work — they're about to start dance class here at the resort, and I don't want to be late! LET'S GO!"

A GRAND GALA EVENING

After the editorial meeting, I went to my office, ready to **dig in** to work. But after a few minutes, I heard a horn honking outside.

I looked out the window — holey cheese! It was Thea on a *motorcycle*!

"Gerrykins, I'm going to get ready for tonight's Grand Gala. Remember to pick up your **tuxedo**."

"Huh?!" I squeaked. "T-tuxedo? Wh-what gala?!"

Thea rolled her eyes. "Don't be a cheesebrain! It's the *Mouseum Gala*!"

Moldy mozzarella! I had totally **FORGOTTEN** that the mouseum was going to receive the prestigious **Petrified Cheese Prize** that evening!

Remember your tuxedo!

9

THE PETRIFIED CHEESE PRIZE

The Petrified Cheese Prize is a prestigious award that is given to the best mouseums in the world. It's very difficult to attain: the mouseum's collection must pass the test of Ratmund Rattisford, esteemed expert in history and archaeology.

I had also **FORGOTTEN** that that evening, the mouseum would officially become the **Archaeology Mouseum of New Mouse City**, expanding to host artifacts from many historic periods. (Until then, it had only been the Egyptian Mouseum.) And I had **FORGOTTEN** that I had been invited to the ceremony!

So I asked Mousella to pick my tuxedo up from the dry cleaner's. Meanwhile, I worked through my own to-do LIST . . .

At 6:00 p.m. on the dot, I returned home.

I responded to 14 emails.

I looked for my invitation to the gala.

I approved 327 drafts to send to press.

I signed a stack of 123 contracts.

I ordered a taxi.

I made 120 phone calls.

Soon, the doorbell **rang**. It was Thea, Trap, Benjamin, and Trappy.

Benjamin greeted me enthusiastically. "Hi, Uncle G! Today Trappy and I went to the **amousement park**!"

Trappy continued. "Heya, Geroni*monimo*! The amousement park was a smash! There was a pirate's cave, and we did a treasure hunt with a **map** — look!"

Trap said hello, too. "Hey there, Geroni*mini*!"

I **sighed**. "How many times do I have to tell

Look, a treasure map!

you mice that my name is *Geronimo*?!"

"Alrighty, Geroni*mation*, if you say so . . ."

"G-E-R-O-N-i-M-O!"

"As you wish . . . but now let's get a move on, or we'll be late to the gala, Geroni*meister*!"

Rat-munching rattlesnakes! Trap would never change.

We arrived at the **mouseum**. There was already a huge crowd waiting to enter, including the mayor!

"My little bat wing! Yooo-hoooo!"

Oh no . . . I recognized that squeak. Alas, I knew it quite well. **Creepella** came at me with open arms.

"My darling mouse, you're here! This mouseum

is beautiful — it would be the perfect place for a wedding, don't you think?"

"A w-w-wedding?!" I stammered.

Creepella chuckled. "Of course! See how perfectly gloomy it would be among all those mummies?!"

Thea chimed in — she's one of Creepella's best friends. "Oh, Creepella! You are so right. It would be perfect for a wedding!"

My eyes opened wide. "Who is getting married?"

Trap piped up, too. "You are truly a special rodent: fascinating, intelligent, classy . . .

Thea, Creepella, and Flora have been friends since their school days. Now my sister, Thea, is a special correspondent for *The Rodent's Gazette*, Creepella is a journalist in Mysterious Valley, and Flora is an herbalist.

just like me! Not like my cousin Geroni*moid*. He's such a fool! Any mouse would be lucky to marry you."

Great chunks of cheddar! Suddenly, it was clear to me . . .

♥ **Trap** ♥
♥ **had a crush** ♥
♥ **on Creepella!** ♥

Trap continued squeaking. "Let's be honest: you need a class-A rat, not just anyone! You need a fascinating, athletic mouse who has seen the **world** and knows what it means to work hard! Did I ever tell you about my **sixteen jobs**?!"

Trappy took out her notebook and cried, "I know them! I've written them all down here*!"

* Do you want to know what Trap's sixteen jobs are?
Just turn the page!

TRAP'S SIXTEEN JOBS

2) Dentist for carnivorous plants

1) Builder of mirror mazes for amusement parks

3) Stuntmouse for dangerous movie scenes

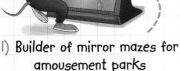

4) Painter of rabbit hutches

5) Flea-circus trainer

6) Writer of messages on the inside of chocolate wrappers

7) Talking mime

8) Mouse responsible for warning others when public benches have been freshly painted

FRESH PAINT

9) Splitter of coconuts

10) Expert guide to shortcuts in New Mouse City

BENVENUTI IN AUSTRALIA

11) Supervisor of potato chip crunchiness

12) Extra in tourist photos (he poses in front of the monuments)

13) Tester of bathroom air fresheners

14) Professional bag packer

15) Mattress tester

16) Baby-chick-sitter

GET THAT REPTILE OFF ME!

Just then, Cyril B. Sandsnout, the director of the mouseum, arrived.

"Geronimo, my dear mouse!" he said. "What a pleasure to have you here on this very special occasion!" Cyril's eyes were sparkling. He was truly excited! He continued squeaking. "We worked really hard all these years, and in the end, our **DREAM** has come true!"

I must confess, his joy really moved me! I smiled and put a paw on his shoulder. "You have truly earned the **Petrified Cheese Prize**!" I said.

"Thank you, friend!" He

CYRIL B. SANDSNOUT

He is the director of the Egyptian Mouseum of New Mouse City.

shook my **PAW**.

Holey cheese,
what a special day! The
Petrified Cheese Prize
was so prestigious,
it would make **New
Mouse City** a great cultural destination for mice
around the world. I was so proud to live in the
fabumouse New Mouse City!

Thanks, friend!

Congratulations!

I entered the mouseum and looked around.
There were artifacts from all through history.
Manuscripts, statues, and even bizarre objects,
like:

- a slipper that belonged to Queen Marie
  Antoinette
- a whisker curler from the sixteenth
  century
- King Louis XV's underwear
- one of Napoleon's socks

Answer: Trappy is hidden in the Viking Room.

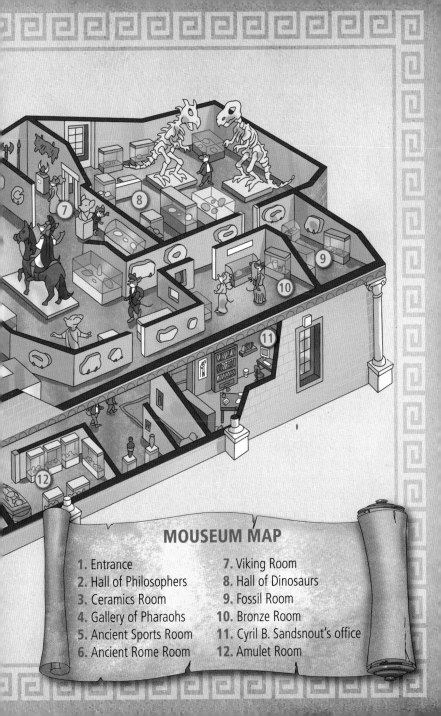

MOUSEUM MAP

1. Entrance
2. Hall of Philosophers
3. Ceramics Room
4. Gallery of Pharaohs
5. Ancient Sports Room
6. Ancient Rome Room
7. Viking Room
8. Hall of Dinosaurs
9. Fossil Room
10. Bronze Room
11. Cyril B. Sandsnout's office
12. Amulet Room

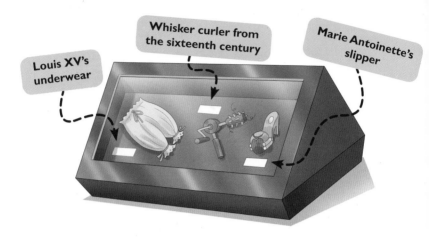

Louis XV's underwear

Whisker curler from the sixteenth century

Marie Antoinette's slipper

Rancid ricotta! What funny relics!

Trappy went up to the nearest display cases to take some PHOTOS , and Benjamin followed her. Trap left with the crew from the show he runs so he could create a special edition show about the event.

Meanwhile, we all waited for the rat who would **award** the prize.

I began to wander around the mouseum — it was fabumouse! Who knew how long it took Cyril to get his paws on all those artifacts!

At one point, I felt a paw tap me on the back, and heard a squeak. *"Pssst!* Geroni*meeny!"*

"Yes? What is it?" I said. As I turned around,

I glimpsed over my shoulder . . .

AAAAAAHHHH!
There was a snake on me!

Why, why, why does everything always happen to me?

I began to flail around, trying to get the snake off me. "Heeeeelp!" I **yelled**. "Pleeeease! Back that reptile on me! Er, I mean: get that reptile off my baaaack!"

Yes? What is it?

Ahhhhh! A snake!

After it dropped off, I scurried away to **HIDE** behind a statue. I was causing such a scene, everyone was looking at me and whispering:

"That disturbed rat is Geronimo Stilton!"

"Isn't he the famous **editor** of *The Rodent's Gazette*?"

"They say that his grandfather was forced to give him the business . . ."

"Ahh, I see — he really is a **STRANGE** one!"

"Look where he's hiding!"

Luckily, Benjamin finally managed to stop me. He waved the **snake** in front of my snout — and I realized that it was made of **rubber**!

Hee, hee, hee!

Put your paw here!

I turned and saw Trap and Trappy chuckling together. That's when I knew they'd played a **prank** on me!

"That snake was you!" I squeaked at Trap, annoyed.

It's better if I stay here!

No, I'll hide here!

He shrugged and replied, "Maybe no, maybe yes — I won't tell! You'll have to guess!"

Thea burst out laughing. "Oh, G! It was just a rubber snake. You're such a **SCAREDY-MOUSE**!"

Trap turned toward Creepella and whispered, "Did you see what a cheesebrain Geronimo is, my darling mouse? You're smart, and you need a courageous rat . . . someone like me!

What a cheesebrain!

My poor little bat wing!

THREE ARTIFACTS ARE MISSING!

Finally, Professor *Ratmund Rattisford* arrived to deliver the Petrified Cheese Prize. He was very serious, and he was accompanied by two **ENORMOUSE, MUSCULAR RODENTS**.

Moldy mozzarella! The Petrified Cheese Prize was so **valuable** that it required two bodyguards!

Ratmund Rattisford approached Professor Sandsnout and looked him up and down while

carefully adjusting the **monocle** over his right eye.

Without a squeak, he clapped his paws, and one of the bodyguards gave Professor Sandsnout the award. Finally, Ratmund Rattisford **CLEARED** his throat and said, "Here is the singular accolade that you have been awarded for recognition of the labor undertaken in this establishment of historical knowledge."

Everyone watching looked at one another, **confused**, but then burst into applause.

Benjamin WHISPERED, "What did Professor Rattisford say?"

I responded with a smile. "He said, 'Here is the special prize for the work you've done at this mouseum.' Rattisford's manner of speech was quite *formal* and a bit OLD-FASHIONED!

Meanwhile, Professor Sandsnout thanked Rattisford and reached out a paw — but Rattisford did not shake it.

Professor Sandsnout was upset but tried to move on. "Um, please follow me for a **GUIDED TOUR** of the —"

But Rattisford lifted his paw and said, "Your suggestion is unnecessary; it goes against my intentions to accept the gesture of companionship. My longing hence is for solitude in my perusal of the artifactual treasures*."

Trappy burst out laughing. "Ha, ha, ha! Listen to how strangely that rat talks!"

"**I understood him quite well!**" Trap said arrogantly. Then he turned to Creepella and said, "I am a very cultured mouse, you see! I can tell you exactly what Rattisford said. It is, um, that . . . he's going to try to be an **architect** of treasure. And I have to say, he's in the right place for that, since we're in a very grand building now!"

---

* In regular speech, this translates to: *I don't need a tour, and don't want anyone to come with me at all. I'd like to go by myself to look at the artifacts.*

"What?! That's not what he said!" I squeaked.

"Well, aren't you particular, Geroni*moomoo*," Trap replied. "All right, then: what did he say?"

He didn't say that!

Pshh!

"My name is *not* Geronimoomoo!" I protested. "Anyway, he said that he doesn't need any help, and he wants to tour the **Mouseum** alone."

Trap rolled his eyes, mimicking me. "'And he wants to tour the mouseum alone' . . . how would you even know that?!"

Meanwhile, Ratmund Rattisford had already left the gallery to explore. Then we heard a yell: "*Abominable**! Three artifacts are missing!"

---

* This means: *Terrible!*

WE NEED A DICTIONARY!

Everyone rushed over to Ratmund Rattisford. He looked very serious. "The mouseum is incomplete! Three more relics are needed!" he squeaked.

Cyril B. Sandsnout approached, confused. "Which ones? How? Where?"

"There, **there**, and **there**," Rattisford replied, pointing to three different spots. He moved

Ouch! My neck!

so fast, I strained my neck trying to see where he was pointing!

"But . . . I don't understand . . ." Professor Sandsnout said.

Rattisford drew himself up and explained. "There are three time periods that do not have an artifact representing them. They are **ancient Greece** between 350 and 300 BC, the Caribbean during the late 1500s, and Europe between 1750 and 1800!"

"Oh no!" Professor Sandsnout cried in shock.

Rattisford was not finished. He pointed a finger at the poor professor and said, "I had heretofore considered you a sincere citizen, yet henceforth I know you as nothing but a reprobate. Ratmund Rattisford will not be hoodwinked! Your collection is incomplete! Therefore, this will be repossessed*!"

Whaaat?

Give it to me!

* In regular speech, this means: *I thought you were an honest rat, but now I see you're a scoundrel. Ratmund Rattisford will not be fooled! Your collection is incomplete! So I am taking this back!*

He clapped twice, and his bodyguards snatched the prize from Professor Sandsnout's paws!

Rat-munching rattlesnakes!

I tried to step in. "Professor Sandsnout has worked so hard to expand the mouseum's collection," I said. "I'm sure that if you give him a chance, he'll find artifacts for those time periods!"

Rattisford raised an EYEBROW and said, "Thus shall it be: it will not be said that Ratmund Rattisford refuses to bestow opportunity! You have two cycles of the earth to find the precious articles, after which I will return*."

Trap, impatient, exclaimed, "Enough with these big words! I can't take it anymore! We need a dictionary!"

Hearing that, Rattisford turned sharply to the crowd. My cousin raised his paws as a sign of innocence and pointed at me. "He was the rat

---

* In regular speech, this means: *So it will be: don't say that Ratmund Rattisford doesn't give second chances! You have two days to find the artifacts before I come back.*

who spoke! It was him! Geroni*moko* Stilto*noko*!"

I sputtered, **exasperated**, "It wasn't me! And, my name is *not* Geronimoko! It's Stilton, Geronimo Stilton!"

"Geronimo Stilton, eh?" Rattisford said. "I will certainly remember you! We will see each other in two cycles of the earth!"

And at that, he left the mouseum.

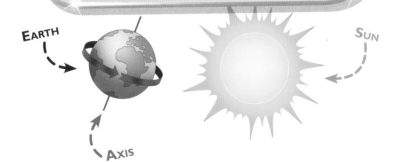

What did Ratmund Rattisford mean by "two cycles of the earth"?

Simple! Each day, the earth takes twenty-four hours to turn completely around on its axis. As our planet spins, different parts of its surface face the sun, and that's why we have day and night. So "two cycles" means "two days."

EARTH

SUN

AXIS

DO WE HAVE TO GO DOWN THERE?!

Ratmund Rattisford left, and the rest of the GUESTS slowly went home. Soon, just Thea, Trap, Creepella, Benjamin, Trappy, and I were there with Professor Sandsnout.

"I'm sorry, friend!" I said to him. "You worked so hard to make this museum special. It can't end this way!"

Professor Sandsnout had a strange look in his eyes as he replied, "Maybe there's something to be done! Come! follow me!"

He went to a statue — and when he bent its arm, the pedestal it was on moved, making a very loud noise. It revealed a trapdoor, leading to a staircase going underground! It was dark down there.

"Wow! A secret passageway!" Trappy squeaked.

I gulped. "Do we have to go down there?!"

Professor Sandsnout nodded and led the way.

The others followed him, but my paws felt **glued** to the floor. Benjamin noticed and called to me: "Come on, Uncle G! You don't want to be left behind!"

Cheese niblets! I was soooo scared!

Why, why, why
does everything
always happen to me?

I stammered, "I-it's j-just that . . . I'm a bit scared of the dark . . ."

"Come on, Geronimo!" Thea called impatiently. "There's nothing to be scared of!"

"Yeah, Geroni*mush*!" Trap added. "Don't let it upset you. Don't think about that time when we were mouselings and I scared you by jumping out from inside a box with my snout covered in white powder! And don't think about when we went to the movies and you thought we were seeing a comedy — but it was a horror film. And don't think about when I hid under your bed and scratched at the ground with fake witch nails. And don't think ab —"

"Enough!" I shouted. Then I went down the stairs.

The stairway became a *labyrinth* suspended in midair. It branched and turned, and there were no walls!

...when I popped out of the box to scare you!

...when I took you to the movies to see a horror film!

...when I scratched the ground with fake witch nails!

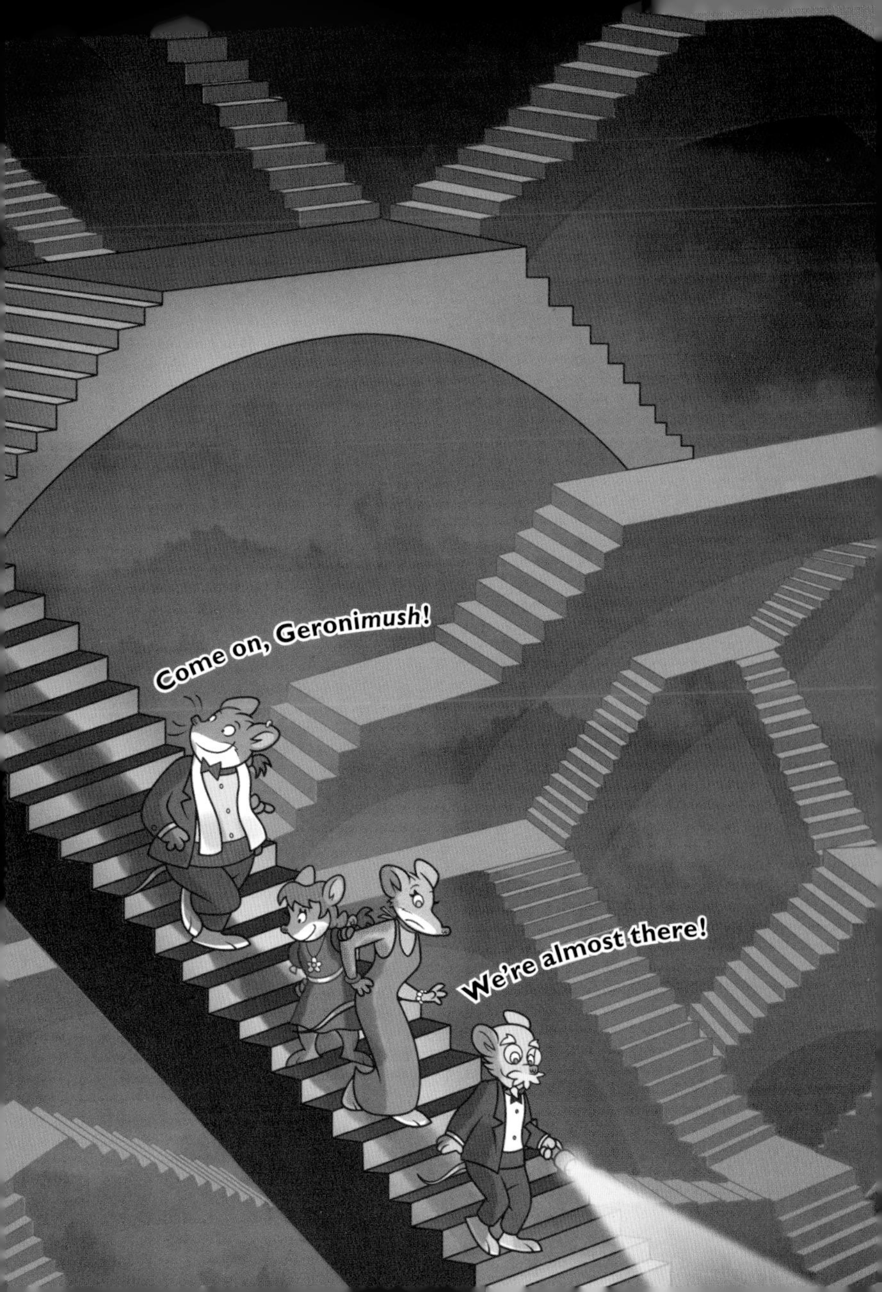
Come on, Geronimush!
We're almost there!

Benjamin and Trappy loved it. "It's just like an amousement park!"

"It's a magnificently chilling atmosphere!" Creepella agreed.

To fight my fear, I chanted over and over: "I am not a scaredy-mouse . . . I am not a scaredy-mouse . . ."

But there was nothing to be done. My whiskers trembled in fright. **WHAT A TERRIFYING SITUATION!**

Finally, after so many flights of stairs going up and down and up and down and up and down, we were in front of a **DOOR** with a plaque on it. I shivered and said, "Umm, do you think we should get out of here? I don't want to disturb whoever is in there . . ."

But Professor Sandsnout responded, "Oh no, Geronimo — they're **waiting** for us inside!"

"They're waiting for us?!" I repeated, shocked. "Who?!"

Professor Sandsnout pressed a **button**, and the doors slid open . . .

SWWIIISSSSHHH!

THE TIME
TRAVELERS' ACADEMY

We entered, and . . . surprise!

We were greeted by three mice I knew well. First was Professor Paws von Volt, a great inventor and my companion on many fun adventures through time. Next was **Bluster Squeak**, a famouse scholar — and my old high school history teacher, who, even now, never missed a chance to quiz me! And finally, there was **Beaker Poirat**, a truly genius scientist. He's also related to HERCULE POIRAT, the greatest detective in New Mouse City!

They all greeted me in unison: "Welcome, Geronimo!"

"Professor von Volt!" I exclaimed. "And Beaker Poirat and Professor

Squeak! Why are you all here?!"

They exchanged glances. Professor von Volt responded for everyone. "Well, Geronimo, we're all here in Beaker's lab because we've founded an important historical and scientific academy."

Cheese and crackers! That was surprising. "An academy?" I asked.

Professor von Volt nodded and announced, "Yes, the Time Travelers' Academy! We even have our own CHARTER! Look!"

THE TIME TRAVELERS' ACADEMY CHARTER

PHILOSOPHY

The Time Travelers' Academy has been created with the goal of uniting all travelers who have been part of or will ever be part of a journey through time. The qualities needed in a time traveler are loyalty, courage, and respect for history.

MEMBERS OF THE ACADEMY

FOUNDING MEMBERS

Beaker
Poirat

Paws
von Volt

Bluster
Squeak

HONORARY MEMBERS

✔ Geronimo Stilton
✔ Thea Stilton
✔ Benjamin Stilton
✔ Trappy Stilton
✔ Trap Stilton
✔ Creepella von Cacklefur

NEW MEMBERS

✔ ....
✔ ....
✔ ....
✔ ....

THE TIME TRAVELER'S VOW

1) I will respect the passage of time on all my journeys.

2) Each trip I take will have a precise and honest objective.

3) I will help the rodents I encounter in any time period.

4) I will take care of my travel companions.

5) I will try to live in harmony with my travel companions.

6) I will never steal anything from the time periods I visit.

7) I will only accept artifacts when they are gifts, and I will always give something in exchange.

8) I will work to know and respect the cultures with which I come into contact.

9) I will be an ambassador of respect, peace, and tolerance.

10) I will respect the time machine that was entrusted to me and I will bring it home intact.

Here are all the time machines we've used so far!

1) The Mouse Mover 3000: traveled to prehistory, Egypt, and medieval Europe

2) The Rodent Relocator: traveled to ancient Rome, the Mayan Empire, and Versailles during the reign of the Sun King

3) The Paw Pro Portal: traveled to the Ice Age, ancient Greece, and Florence during the Renaissance

4) The Tail Transporter: traveled to Cleopatra's time, Genghis Khan's time, and Queen Elizabeth I's time

5) Whisker Wafter: traveled to Napoleon's time, the Vikings' time, and King Solomon's time

6) Cheese-O-Sphere: traveled to prehistory, ancient Troy, the time of the Huns, Charlemagne's time, and the discovery of America

7) Time Tentacle 2000: traveled to ancient Greece, the mythical city of Atlantis, and the creation of Stonehenge

8) ???: What will be the next time machine, and where in time will we travel?

I couldn't believe it: we were honorary members of the Time Travelers' Academy! How exciting!

Beaker chimed in. "**Pungent pistachios!** You must know what we're getting ready for: another adventure through time! We need to help our friend Cyril B. Sandsnout get his Petrified Cheese Prize. We must find THREE ARTIFACTS from the time periods that are missing from the mouseum's collection!"

Beaker stuffed his paw into the pocket of his lab coat, took out a fistful of **pistachios**, and shoved them in his mouth all at once. He chewed them in a flash, smacked his lips, and said, "**MMM! PISTACHERRIFIC!**"

Munch! Munch!

Great Gorgonzola! Beaker was just like his

54

cousin Hercule, except he loved pistachios instead of BANANAS!

Beaker headed toward a doorway to another room in the laboratory that I hadn't seen amid the many **SHELVES**, notebooks and scraps of paper strewn about, books stacked on the floor, scientific equipment, and *COMPUTERS*.

"I knew that you'd be coming, so I tidied up a bit," Beaker said. "I did a pretty good job, if I do say so myself!"

A pretty good job?! Thundering cat tails, that place was a DISASTER!

We all reached the next room and found ourselves on a balcony that overlooked an enormouse machine.

Beaker announced, "Introducing . . . the Bananacraft!"

NAME: Bananacraft
INVENTOR: Beaker Poirat
INSPIRATION: Hercule Poirat (his cousin)
PASSENGERS: Five mice + one guest
LENGTH: Twenty mousemeters (One mousemeter is equal to three rat paws)

THE BANANACRAFT

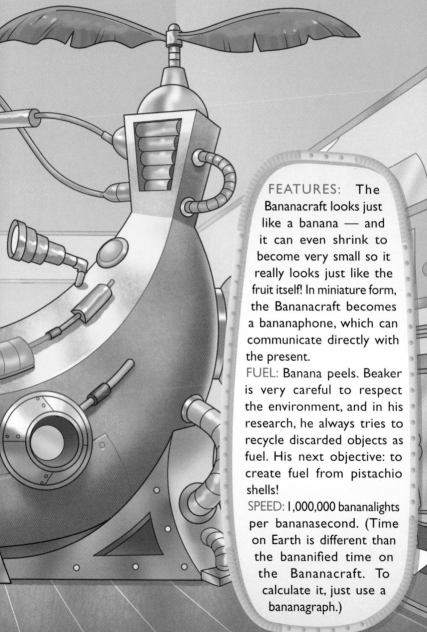

FEATURES: The Bananacraft looks just like a banana — and it can even shrink to become very small so it really looks just like the fruit itself! In miniature form, the Bananacraft becomes a bananaphone, which can communicate directly with the present.

FUEL: Banana peels. Beaker is very careful to respect the environment, and in his research, he always tries to recycle discarded objects as fuel. His next objective: to create fuel from pistachio shells!

SPEED: 1,000,000 bananalights per bananasecond. (Time on Earth is different than the bananified time on the Bananacraft. To calculate it, just use a bananagraph.)

INSIDE THE BANANACRAFT

EVERYTHING IS IN THE SHAPE OF A BANANA:
the BANANASCREEN, a giant screen that goes around
the whole ship and lets you immerse yourself in virtual reality,
practically living in whatever you see projected;
BANANASEATS (WITH SEAT BELTS); the BANANAPILOT, the
control panel for driving and steering the time machine;
the onboard BANANAPHONE, a telephone that puts you
in touch with the Time Travelers' Academy in the
present (Beaker, Paws, and Bluster).

BANANANTENNA:
a high-powered satellite
dish that can receive and
transmit data.

BANANATRANSPORTER:
a transporter that allows
travelers to dematerialize
and rematerialize in another
time period, already dressed in
the proper clothing and with
proper fur-styles for the time.

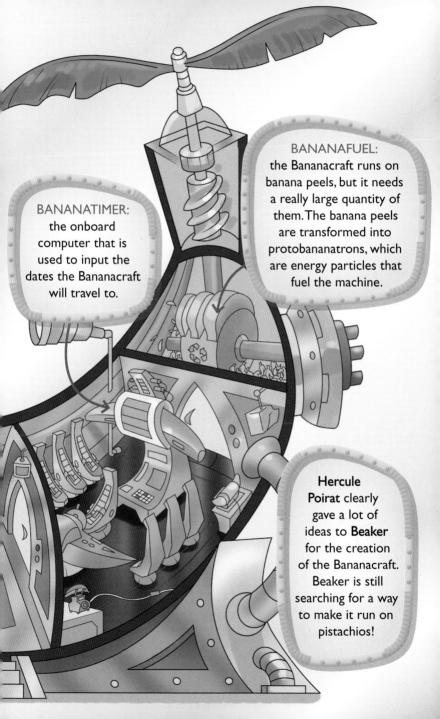

THREE . . . TWO . . . ONE . . . WE WERE OFF!

The crew on this next MOUSERIFIC MISSION through time would be composed of Trap, Creepella, Benjamin, Trappy, and me. Thea would stay in NEW MOUSE CITY and run *The Rodent's Gazette* in my absence.

Come on, let's go in!

Wow!

How cool!

Creepella winked at Thea and said, "Don't worry: I'll keep an eye on my Geronimo!"

I sighed. When Thea and Creepella got together, it always spelled trouble (for me)!

Professor von Volt said, "Before leaving, you need to assign a captain."

"**Me! Me! OBViOUSLY, Me!**" Trap yelled, waving his paw. Then he turned toward Creepella and bragged, "At the end of the day, I'm the only one here with any charm, authority, or athleticism. I will be a **perfect captain!**"

We all got settled in the Bananacraft, each sitting in our own bananaseat. Professor Bluster Squeak typed the **dates** of our destinations into the bananatimer: 300 BC, the 1500s, and the 1700s.

Bluster pointed at me **THREATENINGLY** and said, "Geronimo, there's no time to **quiz you** now, but I'm scheduling a test for when you return." He never could let go of being my history teacher! He continued. "And remember: you only have two days to come back with the three artifacts — otherwise it will be too late, and you will FAIL! Understood?"

The doors closed, the machine's motor started (with an incredible banana smell), and . . .

THREE . . . TWO . . . ONE . . . WE WERE OFFFFFFF!

ALEXANDER THE GREAT'S BIRTHDAY

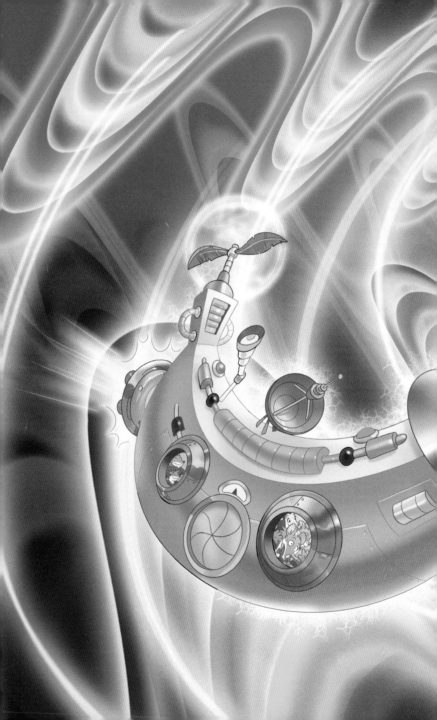

I Don't Feel Fantastic . . .

We were about to arrive in 336 BC, the year that Alexander the Great became king. The Bananacraft zoomed through time at bananalightspeed. It swayed as if we were sailing on a boat at grade 9 wave levels. Everyone else seemed excited . . . but my snout was green with nausea, and I was terrified! I suffer from **SEASICKNESS**. (You knew that, right?) Plus, I didn't feel totally comfortable all closed up in the Bananacraft!

I tried to stand and go to the bathroom,

WAVE SCALE

The conditions of the sea are measured based on the height of the waves with what is called the Douglas scale:

Grade 0: **Calm**
Grade 1: **Nearly calm**
Grade 2: **Smooth**
Grade 3: **Slight**
Grade 4: **Moderate**
Grade 5: **Rough**
Grade 6: **Very rough**
Grade 7: **High**
Grade 8: **Very high**
Grade 9: **Phenomenal**

but the Bananacraft kept **JUMPING**.

Slimy Swiss cheese, it was scary! And I also suffer from *airsickness*. (You knew that, too, right?)

Suddenly, a HOLOGRAM of Beaker appeared in the middle of the room. He was contacting us directly from New Mouse City!

Beaker stared at me and said, "Stilton, you're as **pale** as mozzarella! Are you all right?" He took a handful of pistachios from his pocket and gobbled them up in one bite. Then he explained, "I forgot to tell you that the **Bananacraft** travels on the passage of `time`, which is much like the ebb and flow of waves. That's why it feels

The Bananacraft travels on the passage of time!

TIME

Time is a progression of moments, a bit like music, which is a succession of notes. The Bananacraft travels on the "waves of time."

like being on a boat! The only other thing I have to say is have a good trip, my friends!"

After that, Beaker disappeared. Trappy piped up. "Hey, crew, I had an idea: during our trip, we can keep a detailed **onboard diary**. We can all write down the things we know about the time periods we are visiting! What do you think?"

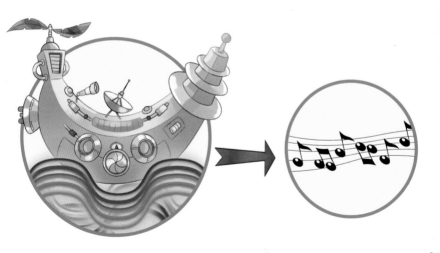

I'll begin! A little while ago in school, I studied **Alexander the Great**! In Greek, the name *Alexander* means "defender of men."

Alexander was born in Pella, Macedonia, in 356 BC. He was the son of Philip II, who was the king of Macedonia, and Olympias. He claimed to be descended from the demigod Heracles on his father's side and the hero Achilles on his mother's side. Olympias wanted to give her son a Greek education, including philosophy and science, to help prepare him to be a great king, so in 343 BC, she called on the great philosopher Aristotle to teach him.

Olimpias

As Alexander became more successful, he even claimed that he was actually the son of the god Zeus!

--- Zeus

At just sixteen years old, Alexander was temporarily entrusted with governing Macedonia in his father's absence. Upon his father's death, he became king at twenty years old.

Alexander the Great

He has gone down in history as Alexander the Great, considered one of the most famous conquerors of all time. In just twelve years of rule, he conquered the Persian Empire, stretching his own empire into Egypt and Asia, including areas that are today Pakistan, Afghanistan, and northern India. He colonized these regions, spreading Greek culture, language, and philosophy.

Rome

Pella

Black Sea

Caspian Sea

Alexandria, Egypt

Indian Ocean

Alexander's Empire

Alexander the Great's Giant Army

Alexander enjoyed sports and physical activity his whole life, and was a skilled athlete and a fierce adversary. Even after he was crowned king, he fought alongside his

soldiers in war. He had the gift of being able to motivate them through the speeches he gave to his troops (which were recounted by others, such as the Roman historian Quintus Curtius Rufus).

One unique trait of Alexander's army was the further development of the phalanx formation, which is a block of foot soldiers standing shoulder to shoulder, equipped with long spears called sarissas. This formation was introduced during Philip's time.

Fun fact:
Alexander's army was followed by bematists (from the Greek word *bema*, which means "step"), men whose job it was to count how many footsteps they took, to measure the distance the army traveled.

YOU'RE ALL DISCOMBOBULATED!

With a loud screech, the Bananacraft stopped sharply.

THUNNNKKK!

Trap unbuckled his seat belt and got up and stretched. "**Yaaaawn!** All of this chatter about Alexander the Great makes me sleepy . . ."

We headed toward the bananatransporter and all positioned ourselves on a platform under some strange-looking pods.

"These look kind of like **showers!**" Benjamin giggled.

I was struck with panic. "What if we don't rematerialize?!" I squeaked.

Trappy answered, "What if we materialize all **scattered** about: with our feet where our

heads should be, or an arm where our leg should be, or a tail instead of a nose . . ."

I turned as *pale* as a Brie rind.

Creepella put a paw on my shoulder and said, "My dear sweet cheese, just stay calm. I'm here to keep an eye on you."

Rat-munching rattlesnakes! H-how could I stay calm at a time like this?! My throat got dry.

Gulp!

Suddenly, a bright ray of banana-yellow light surrounded each of us.

I felt a strange sensation, as if an army of ants were walking all over me . . .

Up and down and up

and down, and up and down and
up and down and up and down and
up and down and up and down and up and
down and up and down and up and down . . .

I looked at my paws and saw that they were **disappearing**.

"HEEEEELPPPPP!"

Then I heard dear Benjamin's reassuring voice from far away:

"It's okayyyy, Uncleeee!"

I turned and saw that he was **disappearing**, too.

Not long after that, we found ourselves in the middle of a **FiELD**, all dressed in Greek tunics.

Trap looked at me with wide eyes and yelled, **"AAAHHH!** Geroni*momo*, you're all discombobulated! You've got an ear

where your snout is, a mouth on your forehead, an eye on your cheek . . ."

Everyone looked at me and cried out. In full panic, I ran to look at my reflection in a nearby pond . . .

Luckily, I was still me! Phew!

Trap snickered, holding his belly. "Ha, ha, ha! You fell for it, you old cheddarhead!"

GERONIMO, YOU ARE HOPELESS!

I was about to protest, but the air around us began to tingle as if electricity was running through it. Suddenly, **Bluster Squeak** materialized right next to us!

"Professor! What are you doing here?!" I exclaimed. "You're not even a hologram — you're here in the fur and whiskers!"

"Are you surprised, Stilton?" he responded. "I decided to come help you using the laboratory's dematerializer. Modestly speaking, I am a great expert in history! I can help you find Alexander the Great, who, during this time, should be about twenty years old. And since we're all here, I can quiz you as well!"

I turned as pale as mozzarella.

"Wh-what do you mean, quiz me?! I'm not ready — I didn't study — there was a fondue stain on that page of my history book! I mean — Professor, I'm not in school anymore!"

Benjamin stepped in. "First things first: we need to get the Bananacraft to a safe place! Look!"

The Bananacraft was on the ground and had shrunk down to miniature size. I was bending over to pick it up when a **dog** ran by, grabbed it, and ran off!

"Stop that dog!" I squeaked.

Stop that dog!

Swiss cheese on a stick — I didn't dare think what would happen if we lost our time machine! We would be stuck forever in the time of Alexander the Great! Plus, the Time Traveler's Vow specified that we were to take care of the time machine!

Trap yelled as loud as he could, "Stop that **fleabag** at once!"

Benjamin added, "Stop that Sweet puppy!"

A young mouse with reddish fur realized what was happening and scurried after the dog, who was running *very fast*.

He caught the dog, retrieved the "banana," and gave it back to us. **Thank goodmouse!**

I put the Bananacraft in my pocket and began to thank the mouseling — and immediately realized that the bananatransporter, in addition to changing our **clothing**, had changed our language. I was squeaking in ANCIENT GREEK!

"Thank you!" I said. "My name is Geronimos, and I come from New Mousiax, a distant **POLIS***."

The young mouse smiled and said, "Nice to meet you, Geronimos. My name is Alexandros!"

* *Polis* means "city" in Greek.

He's so fast!

Stop that sweet puppy!

Ruff, ruff!

I'll get him!

Alexandros . . . that was the Greek way to say *Alexander*! Was this Alexander the Great? This rodent couldn't have been twenty, though — at most, he was THIRTEEN. What a strange coincidence!

Benjamin whispered, "I think this is him . . ."

We all understood what he meant — except for Trap, who said impatiently, "**Huh? Who?!** Tell me! I don't know what you're talking about!"

I whispered, "Alexander the Great!"

My cousin exploded in laughter, screeching, "**The great?!** Ha, ha, ha! He's just a mouseling!"

Bluster nodded. "Interesting clarification, Trap. Indeed, you have always been much smarter than that **slacker** Geronimo. I remember when you were my students: one of you was kind and helpful, and the other — obviously Geronimo — was a cheesebrain!"

Then Bluster turned to Alexandros. "Young

mouse, would you kindly tell me what your **father's** name is?"

Alexandros responded, "Of course! His name is Philip!"

Bluster shoved me and said, "Moldy Manchego, Geronimo! You're hopeless! What DATE did you enter into the bananatimer?! How much do you want to bet that you messed it up? You've always messed up your dates! What am I supposed to do with you?!"

Taken by surprise, I *stammered*, "Um, it s-said 'Pella 343 BC' — er, I think . . . maybe . . ." Then I remembered what had happened and exclaimed,

"Wait a moment, Professor: *you* are the one who **entered** the dates when we boarded!"

He coughed and said, "You always have some excuse ready, don't you, Stilton? You just don't want to admit that you're wrong. Let me tell you what happened! We aren't in 336 BC, we are in 343 BC, seven years before Alexandros is crowned and named 'the great.'"

"You'll always be a cheesebrain!" Trap added. I just shook my snout.

Alexander at 13

Alexander at 20

WHY DON'T YOU ALL COME TO MY HOUSE?

Benjamin and Trappy started playing with a **ball** that Alexandros had brought with him.

> **PLAYING WITH A BALL**
>
> In ancient Greece, children played with balls that were sometimes made of pieces of leather filled with feathers or hair.

"I have an idea," Alexandros said. "Why don't you all come to my house? Today is my **birthday**, and this evening there will be a big party in my honor. My father, Philip, and my mother, Olympias, will be happy to have you as **GUESTS**!"

Benjamin approached me and said under his breath, "Uncle G, I think this is a good chance to find a GREEK ARTIFACT to bring to the mouseum!"

Trap heard and jumped in. "Ah, yes! Like a little **jewel**, or precious stone, or gold! We can nab something, make the Bananacraft bigger, and get going!"

"Oh no, Trap! We can't **steal**!" I objected. "It even says so in the Time Traveler's Vow! We are on a mission to help Professor Sandsnout, not to get rich. I am a gentlemouse, and I always respect the rules."

"Ugh, fine!" Trap said. "You're such a rule follower, Geronimo!"

We all walked toward the royal palace. The sun was high in the sky, but there was a nice wind caressing our **fur**.

We went down the slope of a hill, and though I was tired, I admired the **view**. Cheese niblets, it was so cool to be in Pella in the fourth century BC with one of the most important figures in history, even if he was still a little mouseling. Alexandros would become a great ruler, but he didn't know it yet!

While the young mice were in front of us chatting, Bluster took the opportunity to give me a pop quiz.

"You can't get out of this, Geronimo!" he said. "And I'm warning you: NO CHEATING!"

Luckily, I had listened to dear Benjamin's info

Concentrate!

Argh!

Help Geronimo answer Bluster's questions!

QUIZ

1. When was Alexander the Great born?

2. What is his father's name?

3. What is his mother's name?

4. Who was his teacher?

Answers:
1. 356 BC, 2. Philip II, 3. Olympias, 4. Aristotle

on the Bananacraft, so I passed the quiz.

"I could have failed you, Geronimo, but I'll give you a C-minus. Consider it a grade of encouragement!"

Phew! I had just scraped by.

Soon we saw the **PALACE** ahead of us in the distance.

WELCOME TO PELLA!

Alexandros pointed to the palace of Pella and said, "There's my house!"

Trap's eyes went wide. "Great Gorgonzola! You call that a house?! It's enormouse!"

The palace was truly magnificent. It had columns and statues and beautiful courtyards.

A mouse greeted us at the entrance. She waved her paw elegantly and said, "Welcome to our palace. My name is Olympias, and I am Alexandros's mother." What a fascinating rodent!

"My name is Geronimos, and my family and my friends and I come from New Mousiax," I said, then bowed and gave her a kiss on the paw. (I'm a real gentlemouse!)

Olympias

93

Creepella whispered, "Don't be *too* chivalrous!" Then she approached Olympias, admiring the snake-shaped bracelet she wore.

"How fabumouse! I adore **snakes**!" Creepella said.

"Me too!" Olympias replied. "The more poisonous, the better! Please, come see my snakes!"

I felt faint. "S-*see* your snakes? Wh-what?!" I stammered.

Rancid ricotta! I am dreadfully afraid of snakes!

But Creepella wasted no time accepting, and Olympias led us to her chambers.

I tried to slip away, but Bluster **grabbed** my ear.

"Where do you think you're going, Stilton?" he barked. "A real time traveler never misses an experience! You have always been a **slacker**,

Stop right there!

Squeak!

but I must say that you're getting worse with age. Follow your cousin Trap's example: he is a diligent student!"

Trap smiled at Bluster, but as soon as the professor turned, Trap stuck his **tongue** out at me.

We walked through the luxurious palace. The floors were made of fabumouse mosaics, the walls were covered in lush tapestries, and the halls were lit by **candlelight**.

Creepella exclaimed, "This would be a wonderful place for a wedding! Don't you think, my precious bat wing?"

I didn't even respond. The only thing I could think about were . . . **snakes**!

As Olympias opened the door to her chambers, I tried to make an excuse to leave.

"Umm, I just remembered, I didn't greet

the king! A true gentlemouse always does that. I must find him right aw —"

"There's no rush," Olympias interrupted. "Philip is entertaining other guests. Instead, look at my basket of super-poisonous snakes!"

She grabbed my arm and dragged me to the basket. I tried to get free — and accidentally

knocked over the basket, spilling out the snakes! I don't know what happened next, because I immediately FAINTED.

Awesome!

You'll see how cool the snakes are!

GAME

How many snakes
are in this room?

Answer: *There are ten snakes.*

THE GREAT TEACHER

I came to my senses, of course — or should I say, *by force*, because when I came to, Bluster was **smacking** me on the snout.

"Wake up, Stilton! Come on, now!"

"Huh?" I asked, opening my eyes weakly.

"What happened? I thought I saw a sna —"

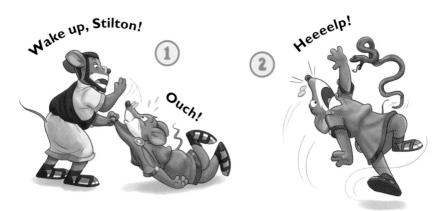

Wake up, Stilton!

Ouch!

Heeeelp!

Bluster was smacking me when I came to!

Then I grabbed something . . . Help! It was a snake! I fainted again.

I felt something holding my tail. Thinking it was Trap's paw, I grabbed it.

"Don't pull my tail, Trap! I'm awake!" I squeaked. But when I lifted my paw, I saw that I had grabbed . . . a **SNaaaake**!

I fainted again.

The second time I was also awakened by force: Trappy poured a bucket of freezing water on me!

Wake up, Uncle G!

(3)

To wake me, Trappy poured a bucket of freezing water on me!

Trap shook his snout. "Ugh! Geroni*mimi*, you're always embarrassing us!"

At that moment, a servant arrived and said, "Your Majesty, we are ready for the prince's FESTIVITIES."

We looked around, but Alexandros was no longer there. Where had he gone?

We searched the palace and found Alexandros walking under a portico with another rodent.

Cheese and crackers, that rat reminded me of someone . . . BUT WHO?!

Olympias smiled. "I should have guessed that he would be here with his teacher," she said. "He cares for him so much!"

"Excuse me, my queen: who is his teacher?" I asked. "He seems familiar . . ."

Bluster PINCHED my ear, making me jump.

Then he whispered, "What do you mean, 'he seems familiar'?! Don't you know who that is?!

Geronimo, you are really a lost cause . . . That's the **philosopher Aristotle**!"

Holey cheese! Bluster was right!

As we saw the teacher and student walk off, I thought about the fact that we were watching not only one of the most heroic future leaders in history, but also one of the greatest philosophers!

Aristotle

Aristotle was an ancient Greek philosopher, scientist, and logician, born in 384 BC. Around 342 BC, he was called to the palace of Pella to give Alexander a classical education. We don't know exactly what he taught Alexander, but the two kept in touch for many years.

What is philosophy? It is a Greek word that means "love of wisdom." Philosophy is the study of knowledge and explores deep questions about existence, knowledge, ethics, and more.

Aristotle was a sharp observer of the world around him. He said: *"Everything that depends on the action of nature is by nature as good as it can be."*

He was the first to sort animals into genus and species based on his observations — a method that scientists built on centuries later.

Aristotle was said to dress in a striking style and wear many rings on his fingers.

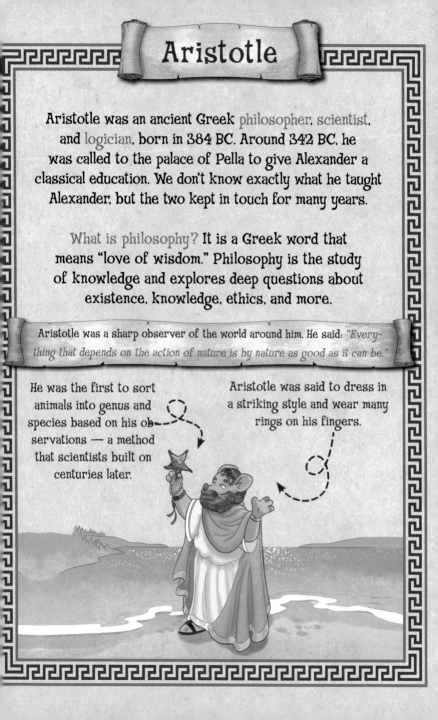

I saw a scroll near me on the ground, so I picked it up. Bluster came and looked over my shoulder as I opened it (he knew how to read ANCIENT GREEK perfectly), and he read aloud, *"Sing, O goddess, the anger of Achilles son of Peleus, that brought countless ills upon the Achaeans . . .* But this is **THE ILIAD***!"

THE ILIAD

Alexander was very passionate about Homer's *The Iliad*, and considered his copy a great treasure. He is even said to have slept with it under his pillow!

"Homer's *The Iliad*?!"

Trap snatched the scroll from my paw. "I bet it's worth quite a bit in our time! We could **take** it and sell it to the mouseum!"

I took the **scroll** back and responded, outraged, "Shame on you, Trap! Not only does

---

* *The Iliad* is an epic poem, which is a long narrative poem that tells of heroic deeds. *The Iliad* tells the story of the Trojan War. It is attributed to the Greek poet Homer.

that go against the Time Traveler's Vow, but it's **DISLOYAL** to Professor Sandsnout!"

"What's the big deal?!" Trap huffed. "It's just a piece of yellowed paper . . ."

Bluster intervened. "I'm sure that Trap meant to say 'leave it.' A **kind** student like him would never steal an artifact! Right, Trap?"

"Of course that's what I meant!" Trap said with an innocent look on his snout. "I'm glad you understand me. My cousin **never** trusts me. Humph!"

LET THE PARTY BEGIN

We all gathered beneath the portico, where the other party guests were.

Olympias announced, "Now the guests will give their birthday gifts to Alexandros."

At that moment, **King Philip** himself arrived. He seemed like a pretty grouchy mouse.

He gave us a SUSPICIOUS look. "And who are you?" he asked. "I've never seen you around these parts. One of you, squeak!"

Trap patted me on the back — **THWACK!** — and I was forced to step forward.

"He'll speak for us!" Trap said.

I STAMMERED, "Um, m-my name is G-Geronimos. We come from New Mousiax."

King Philip approached me, just a few inches from my snout. Was he counting my whiskers?!

"I don't trust mice I don't know . . . and I don't know you!" he said. "Do you know the punishment for being a Persian spy? DO YOU? HUH?"

Putrid Parmesan! I gulped loudly. "We are not Persian spies! Truly! We came to celebrate *mégas** Alexandros."

Hearing that, Philip became silent . . . then exploded in a fit of laughter. "HA, HA, HA, HA, HA! *Mégas?!* Who, him?! Ha, ha, ha! At

---

* In ancient Greek, *mégas* means "great" or "big," and *mikrós* means "small."

most, he is *mikrós**!" he said, turning to his son
and ruffling his fur.

Then Philip said to him, "Now come, open your
gifts."

Alexandros sighed and headed toward the pile
of presents. They were from princes, noblemice,
and other famouse mice . . . but not from any
MOUSELINGS his own age. He opened the
precious gifts one by one, but it didn't seem like he
was having much fun.

Oh, what a nice . . . sculpture.
Thanks — I needed one of these . . .

Gifts
Alexander the Great received

- A golden cup for drinking water
- A little statue of himself
- A pitcher
- A stone sculpture of his snout

- An urn with his face on it
- Another urn that was bigger
- Yet another urn that was truly enormouse
- A stool inlaid with precious stones
- A golden amulet from Egypt

- Money and jewels
- A ladle (made of gold, obviously!)
- A rug embroidered with lions and dragons

Take Us to Go Play!

Benjamin and Trappy also noticed that Alexandros seemed disappointed. They went over to him while the adult mice were talking. Benjamin grabbed his paw and said, "Let's go to your room and **PLAY**! Do you want to?"

Alexandros's face lit up. "**REALLY?**" he asked.

Trappy gave a thumbs-up. "Of course!" she said. "Come on, let's go!"

Taking advantage of the busy, crowded room, the three mice SNUCK OUT without being seen, bringing the gifts with them.

I decided to follow them to make sure that everything was okay. Once I got to Alexandros's room, I saw something that melted my HEART like fondue: the mouselings were playing together, and the birthday mouse was finally HAPPY!

That was the first time since we'd arrived that I'd seen Alexandros laugh like that.

Trap, Creepella, and Bluster soon joined me.

Alexandros saw us at the door and said, "Shall we all play *ephedrismos*? It's a game. Two mice at a time toss stones at a rock on the ground. Whoever loses has to carry his partner while blindfolded until he touches the rock."

TOYS AND GAMES IN ANCIENT GREECE

TOPS: Ancient Greek children liked to play with spinning tops and see who could spin theirs the longest.

YO-YOS: These yo-yos were made of wood, metal, or painted clay.

KNUCKLEBONES: Knucklebones were small bones or game pieces that were thrown like dice. This game was similar to playing modern-day jacks.

DOLLS: Ancient Greek dolls were most commonly made out of clay, and many even had arms and legs that could move on joints.

TOY ANIMALS: These were made out of clay, bronze, or glass, and sometimes were on wheels.

BALL GAMES: Ancient Greek balls were sometimes made of leather and filled with feathers or hair.

HIDE-AND-SEEK: Played much like we play it today!

SWINGS: These were made with a rope hanging from a tree.

He pointed to a rock in the middle of the room. "Ready?"

Soon, I found myself **blindfolded** with my cousin Trap on my shoulders.

SQUEEEEAK!

Moldy mozzarella! He was so heavy!

Alexandros had Benjamin on his back, and — obviously — he got to the rock before me. After a few moments carrying Trap, I collapsed like a piece of **string cheese**!

Come on, get up!

Aaack!

A MARVEMOUSE GIFT

When we finished the game, Alexandros giggled. "Thank you, friends!" he said. "This has been the best birthday I've ever had. I don't often get to PLAY with mice my own age: the life of a future king can be very lonely at times."

Benjamin nodded, thoughtful. "Maybe it would be good for you to have a friend who you could play with and grow with. Maybe . . . a PET!"

Alexandros smiled. "Actually, my dream is to have my very own horse!"

"Maybe you could call it Bucephalus!" I said, chuckling. I knew that was the name of Alexander the Great's famous horse!

Alexandros loved my idea. "Bucephalus . . . that's nice!" he said.

Benjamin rummaged through the pockets of

his **chiton**,* taking out a print of Bucephalus the horse that he had with him. On our way to ancient Greece on the Bananacraft, he'd printed it on **papyrus** using the bananaprinter, in case it was useful.

Benjamin handed it to Alexandros and said, "This is our gift to you for your birthday, in honor of your future horse!"

Alexandros took the paper. He was moved. "Thank you, friends! This is truly a marvemouse **gift**. Let me repay your generosity." From his pile of gifts, he pulled out a **jar** with his face on it and handed it to Benjamin.

Great Gouda! We had our **ARTIFACT** for the mouseum!

Trap wrinkled his nose. "Couldn't we have some **GOLD** instead?" he asked.

---

* A chiton is a tunic made of linen or wool and worn by the ancient Greeks.

BUCEPHALUS,
Alexander's Horse

A few months after our visit, Alexander saw a horse he thought was fabumouse — it was tall, fast, and lively — but all the other mice thought the horse was too wild to tame. Alexander noticed that the horse was just afraid of its own shadow, so he turned the horse's head to face the sun, to make his shadow disappear. This calmed the horse, and Alexander was able to mount him and tame him. After that, the two were inseparable. Alexander named the horse Bucephalus.

1) Bucephalus was a lively horse. Many thought he was too wild to tame.

2) Alexander noticed that he was just afraid of his own shadow.

3) So he found a way to calm the horse and tame him.

4) That day forged a lifelong bond between them.

I was about to yell at my cousin, when the door to the room burst open. Philip stormed in, leading a group of **SOLDIERS**. The king pointed his finger at us and squeaked, "Stop those Persian spies! They are trying to mousenap the prince!"

Thundering cat tails! "There must be some MISTAKE," I tried to explain. "We've already told you that we're not Persian spies — we're just here to *celebrate* Alexandros!"

Stop those Persian spies!

But Philip responded, "I don't believe you! Tell the truth: you want to mousenap him!"

At that point, I felt a **tug** on my tunic. It was Creepella, who murmured, "I don't think these rats intend to listen to our explanations, my little bat wing. Instead, I think we'd better . . . *RUUUUUUNNNN*!"

Let's go! Get a move on!! Quick! There must be a mistake! Run!

THE BANANACRAFT HAS DISAPPEARED!

We ran through the halls of the palace, looking for a way out. It was a real $LABYRINTH$!

King Philip and his soldiers were on our tails. Rancid ricotta! If they caught us, they would turn us into mouse meatballs!

THE PERSIANS

The Persians were great enemies of the Greeks. The Persian Empire extended across the land east of Greece, and they invaded Greece several times.

MACEDONIA

PERSIAN EMPIRE

MEMBERS OF THE LEAGUE OF CORINTH

Trap looked over at Creepella and proudly clapped a paw to his chest. "I'll save you!" he said. "Not like that cheesebrain Geronimo! Quick, follow me!"

Game

Help Geronimo and his friends get out of the palace of Pella without getting caught!

My cousin turned to the **RIGHT**, then **RIGHT** again, then to the **RIGHT** one more time, and then **RIGHT** again.

At that point, we were back to exactly where we started! Cheese and crackers!

We heard the soldiers arriving . . . there was no time to lose!

Trappy opened the first door we saw and said, *"Quick, let's hide in here!"*

We all ran inside, and then realized we were back in Olympias's chambers . . . which was still covered in **SNAKES**!

I felt my vision blur, my paws sweat, my mouth dry up, my knees give way . . . yes, I was about to **FAINT** again!

Trap yanked me back out into the hall.

"SN . . . SN . . . SNAKES . . ." I murmured, dazed.

My friends ran away, dragging me behind them.

They were going so fast that around one curve, they bonked my head against an **URN**. Slimy Swiss cheese, that hurt!

OUCH, OUCH OUCHIE!

We finally reached the exit. But when I stood up, I realized that something was missing.

"Oh no! I lost the **Bananacraft**!" I squeaked.

I took off my glasses so I could cry. Then Benjamin pointed to something on our right. "Uncle G, here it is! Look!"

We turned, and there was that same little **DOG** from when we arrived in Pella. He again had the

Bananacraft (in miniature form) in his jaws! But, unlike that morning, he didn't seem like he was going to run. He was looking at us and wagging his tail.

"He just wants to play!" Benjamin said, smiling. He picked up a stick from the ground, whistled, and threw it for the dog. "Go get it, little friend!"

The dog immediately dropped the Bananacraft and darted off to get the stick.

"Benjamin, you're a genius!" I exclaimed.

Then I grabbed the time machine and pressed the button to make it bigger.

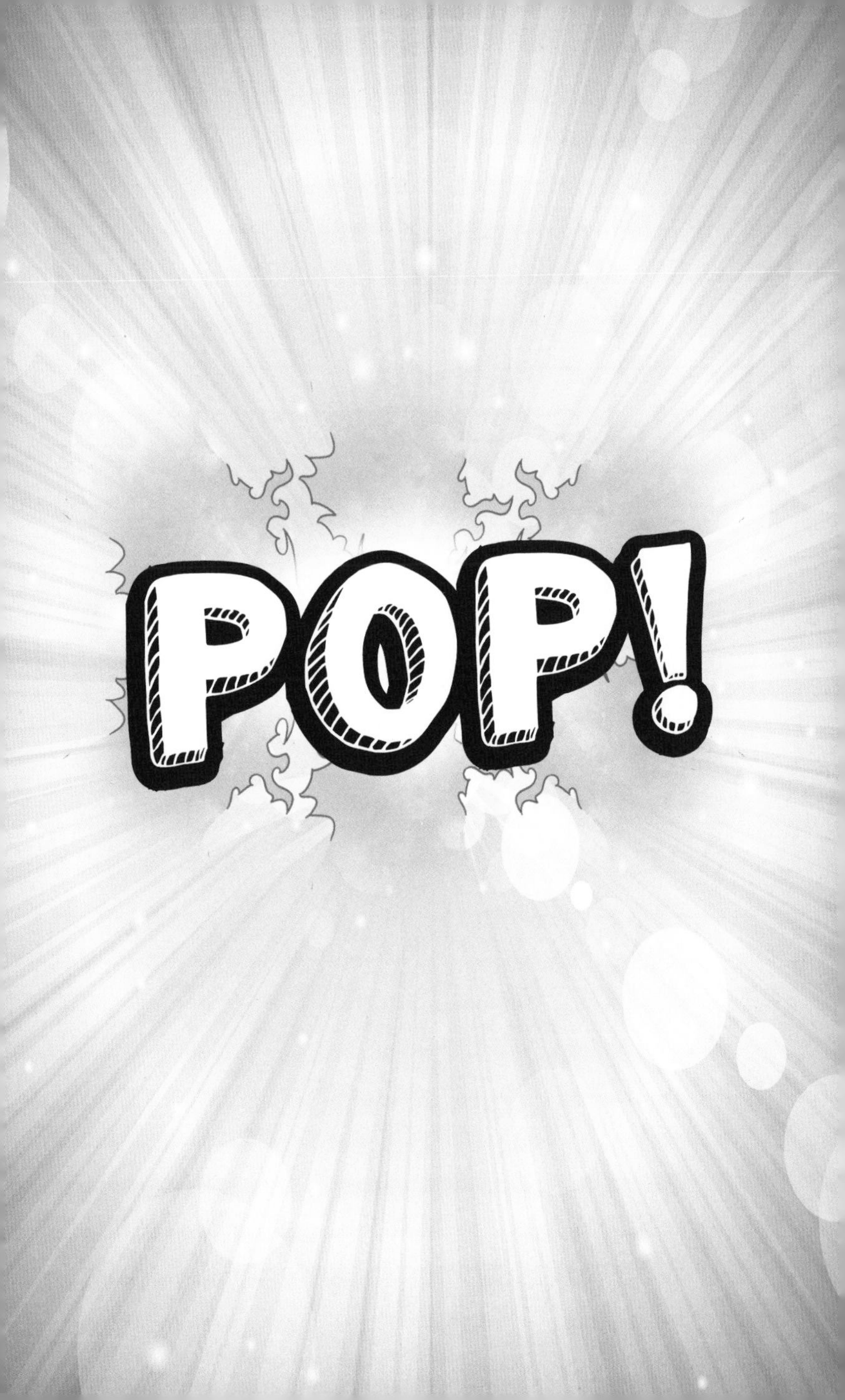
POP!

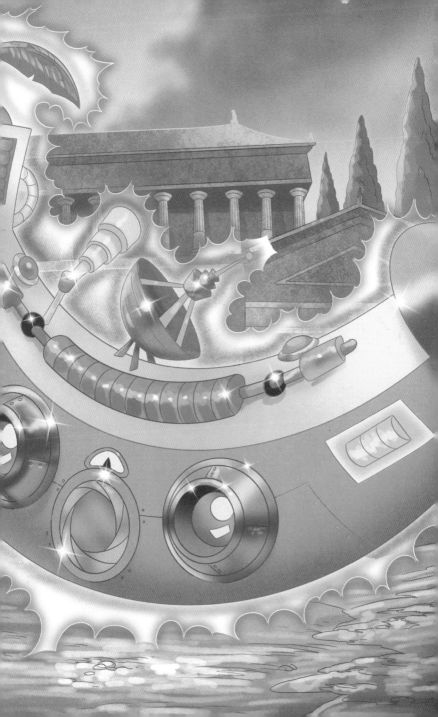

ON BOARD
ONCE MORE

The Bananacraft was in front of us, ready to take us to a new era. Just then we heard a cry from the palace: "There they are! Get those spies!"

It was Philip's soldiers. They had found us!

Come on, enter!

Trap exclaimed, "If you want to save your fur, don't wait any longer! Hurry up!"

Then he SHOVED us so we were all jammed in the Bananacraft doorway tighter than a tube of squeeze cheese . . . until we popped inside.

But our troubles weren't over. When we got inside the Bananacraft, I tripped and accidentally smashed into the controls of the bananatimer with my elbow. The 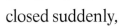 closed suddenly, one moment before the soldiers burst in. The numbers on the bananatimer *spun* around without stopping . . . and the bananatransporter activated!

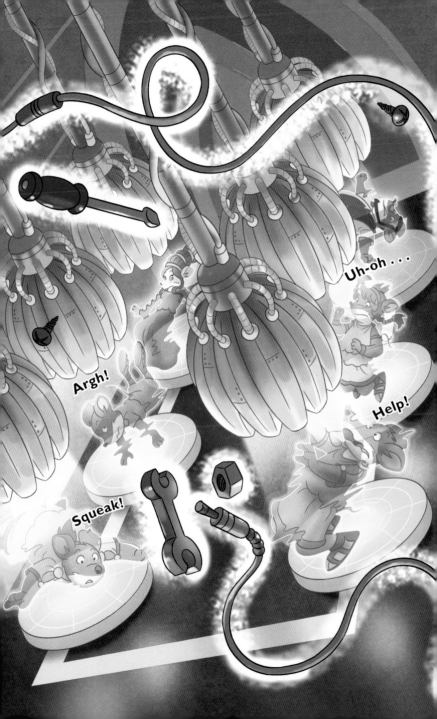

There were a few *jolts*. Then I heard an engine whir, and we were projected once more through time. The only problem was . . .

We didn't know where we were headed!

We were **tosseD** around for what felt like forever . . .

Holey cheese, what was going to happen to us?!

CLEOPATRA'S PALACE

ANCIENT EGYPT

We materialized in a *mousetastic palace* in the middle of a crowd of rodents dressed up in tunics.

Bluster looked at the clothes and said in awe, "Great chunks of cheddar! I think we've ended up in ANCIENT EGYPT!"

Then he looked at me sharply and continued. "Geronimo, you're as **foolish** as ever. Because of you, we've been tossed among the pyramids and papyruses. What do you have to say for yourself?"

Great chunks of cheddar! We're in Egypt!

I barely managed to blurt out my excuse: "B-b-but it wasn't my fault! Trap **pushed** us into the Bananacraft and I, er, tripped and fell into the bananatimer, and —"

"There, you see: you even admit that it's your fault! And don't even try to rope Trap into this!"

I sighed. Every conversation with Bluster Squeak ended up the same way: everything was my fault!

Why, why, why
did everything always happen to me?

Resigned, I picked up the miniaturized Bananacraft. Meanwhile, Trap knelt down at Creepella's feet. "I've never seen such a beautiful Egyptian mouse! Geronimo isn't worthy of a **rodent** like you."

My heart beats for you!

Um . . .

Then he touched the right side of his chest and exclaimed, "*My* **heart** *beats for you!*"

Benjamin coughed and said, "Um, actually, your heart is on the ᴸᴱᶠᵀ side of your chest!"

I approached a nearby rat. "Excuse me, could you please tell me where we are?" I asked.

His **EYES** opened wide. "What do you mean, *where we are*? Are you pulling my tail?!"

I signed and tried again. "No, no! I'm just feeling a little . . . confused at the moment."

"What a strange mouse you are! We are at Queen Cleopatra's palace, of course. She is about to give an official speech!"

A chill went down my tail. I had already met Queen Cleopatra on a previous journey through time,* and I remembered that she was very anxious, unstable, and unpredictable!

But Creepella lit up and exclaimed, "I

---

* Dear rodent readers, do you remember? We met in *Lost in Time: The Fourth Journey Through Time*!

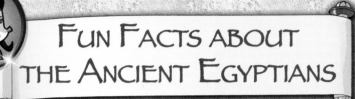
CLOTHING: Ancient Egyptians wore clothing made of linen, a light fabric that is perfect for warm climates. The male rodents wore shirts with loincloths or kilts, and female rodents wore dresses. The rich adorned their clothing with jewelry.

FOOD: Ancient Egyptians ate a variety of food, like bread and cake, meat and fish, beans and vegetables, and fruit. But they only used forks for cooking, not eating!

CLEOPATRA: Cleopatra (69 BC–30 BC) was a very powerful Egyptian queen, who is still very famous today. She knew how to speak many languages and was known to be very charming and intelligent and a great leader. Legend has it that she died from being poisoned by a snake bite.

QUEEN CLEOPATRA

CALENDAR: The Egyptians were the first to invent a logical calendar based on the sun. Their year was made up of 365 days, which were divided into twelve months that were thirty days each, with five extra days added at the end of the year.

JEWELS: Ancient Egyptians wore rings, bracelets, anklets, necklaces, earrings, tiaras, hair ornaments, and more. Among the rich, the most popular type of jewelry was made of gold.

GOLD RING

MUSIC: Music and dance were very important to the ancient Egyptians, and music was present at every type of event. They played instruments including the harp, oboe, flute, trumpet, lute, drums, and tambourine. The sistrum was often used: it was a handheld percussion instrument, usually made of bronze. It had a handle with a U-shaped frame attached that had holes with little poles that went through them. Shaking a sistrum made a rattling noise.

BRONZE SISTRUM

SCHOOL: There were two types of formal schools for privileged male youths in ancient Egypt: one for scribes, and one for those training to be priests. Schools were strict, and discipline could be severe.

MAKEUP: Perfume and makeup were worn by both male and female ancient Egyptians. They outlined their eyes with black or green eye kohl and they used oils, creams, and balms to soften the skin, protect from sunburn, and more.

COSMETICS CASE

TIME: Ancient Egyptians used sundials, or shadow clocks, to tell the time of day based on the location of the shadow created by an elevated piece on the clock when the clock was facing a specific direction in the sun. A small shadow clock was possibly the first portable timepiece invented!

adore Cleopatra! I know all about her and the Egyptians . . ."

Bluster applauded warmly after Creepella's presentation. "Great Gorgonzola, that was sublime! Too bad I never had you as a student, Creepella — it would have given me so much satisfaction!" He shot me a dirty look and continued. "Instead I had to deal with old Stilton over here . . ."

Suddenly, there was a shout. "AAAAAH! Queen Cleopatra has lost her Aspis! If we don't find him, she'll feed us to the royal beasts!"

"ASPIS?" I squeaked. We were all curious. Then I focused on the second part of the shout. "Wait a second . . . the ROYAL BEASTS?! HEEEEEELPPPP!"

Is It a Puppy?

We were all confused, and all started asking questions at once.

"WHO IS ASPIS?"

"Is it a puppy?"

"Maybe it's a friendly dog . . ."

"I don't remember Cleopatra having a pet pup . . ."

Meanwhile, all the other mice present were **worried** and bent over the ground looking for this mysterious Aspis. They really didn't want to become lunch for the royal beasts. Moldy mozzarella! Neither did we!

One rat whispered with a trembling voice, "Let's hope it doesn't bite anyone!"

I turned as PALE as a Brie rind. "*Bite?!*"

Right then, another mouse bumped into me,

and I ended up sprawled across the floor, with my **GLASSES** knocked off.

I felt around to try to find them before someone crushed them — without my glasses I can't see a cheese crumb! Finally I grabbed what I thought was the arm of my glasses, though it was a bit **thick** and soft . . . Strange, very strange!

"I found them!" I squeaked.

"Oh no, Uncle G . . ." Benjamin replied.

What did he mean? Suddenly, Trap shoved

147

my (actual) glasses onto my snout, saying, "Geronimo, you really are a cheesebrain!"

It was then that I saw what I had grabbed. "A SNAAAAKEEE!" I screamed. "Holey cheese, not again!"

Why, why, why does everything always happen to me?

I heard the crowd scream, "Aspis! Aspis! Aspis! That rat found Aspis!"

I fainted. When I opened my eyes, I was facing the royal throne. And looking at me with deep, dark eyes was the fascinating . . .

Queen Cleopatra!

I bowed before her.

The queen lifted an eyebrow and gestured for me to approach.

"Are you the mouse who found my ASPIS?"

I nodded. "Yes, my queen. My name is Geronitep, and I am at your service," I said.

A TRIBUTE TO THE PHARAOH

All across what had been the Persian Empire, from the Mediterranean to the Middle East, cultural practice when greeting another person was to bow and/or kiss hello in different ways, depending on your social rank and the social rank of whoever you were greeting. When greeting a king or pharaoh, you would bow and blow a respectful kiss. This was called *proskynesis*, which means "kissing toward" in Greek.

She studied me for what felt like a long time, then said, "Strange . . . you remind me of a foolish rodent who I met about a year ago. I should have fed him to the royal beasts! You don't easily forget a cheesebrain like that. Do you happen to be a relative of his?"

Cheese niblets! Cleopatra remembered me!

Cheese niblets! She recognized me!

What could I do?! I didn't want to **contradict** her and end up thrown to the royal beasts!

"Um . . . well, actually, I —"

Luckily, Trap ran to my aid. "My queen, he isn't related to that cheesebrain — he's just someone who *resembles* him. A lookalike. I mean, he really is the spitting image, so it's almost like it is the same mouse . . ."

The queen waved her paw to stop him, smiling. "So much squeaking! No matter, the important thing is that you found my **beloved** Aspis: without him I really can't sleep."

I eyed the snake **wrapped** around her arm. I thought, *I wouldn't be able to sleep at all if I knew*

My beloved Aspis!

I HAD A SNAKE NEXT TO ME! Squeak! Just imagining it made me tremble from my whiskers to my tail!

Obviously, though, I didn't say any of that and just smiled at Cleopatra.

The queen continued. "I will not **FEED** you to the royal beasts — at least not today! Tell me: how may I repay your noble gesture?"

Trap butted in at once. "If I may, I do have a tiny idea. I propose you give us, say, a few tiaras, a dozen **golden rings**, a pair of bracelets, twenty necklaces with precious stones, and some **pendants** in the shape of . . . what's that animal you love so much?! Ah yes, the **cockroach**!"

Cleopatra leaped up, offended. "You mean the scarab beetle!"

Before my cousin did any more damage (or ended up being fed to the royal beasts), I started

It's the scarab beetle!

Ah yes, the cockroach!

squeaking. "Don't worry, Your Majesty, we don't want anything in return! It was pleasure enough to meet you — and an even greater pleasure to have helped you!"

I was already trying to drag Trap out of the palace when Cleopatra stopped us.

"**Wait!** Take this! I have another, anyway."

I was frozen with fear. Was she was talking about Aspis?! But when I turned around, I saw that she was holding out . . . *HER SCEPTER!*

I smiled, relieved, and said, "Thank you, Your Majesty! It is a true honor to receive this gift from you!" Great Gouda, how fabumouse!

SCEPTER

In ancient Egypt, the scepter was a symbol of power for both royalty and the gods. A staff that curves at the top like a shepherd's crook was called the hekat and represented the idea that the pharaoh was the shepherd of the citizens.

TIME IS
RUNNING OUT!

We made the Bananacraft bigger and climbed aboard our time machine, saying good-bye to Cleopatra's ANCIENT EGYPT.

We'd ended up there accidentally, but it turned into a fabumouse adventure: we got to see the fascinating queen, and we ended up with a mousetastic artifact! That was a win in my eyes!

I'll take these!

Bluster took Alexander the Great's **urn** and the Queen's **hekat** and approached the bananatransporter.

"I'll take these to the present," he said. "They'll be safer with me in New Mouse City. I don't trust you: you're too distracted and accident-prone!"

"Wait — you're going home already?!" I exclaimed.

WAVING Cleopatra's hekat, Bluster responded, "Of course, Stilton! I've done my bit. I must say, we wouldn't have gotten these artifacts without me! Plus I am a busy mouse — not like a lazyfur I know." He gave me a piercing look and continued. "Try to manage on your own. And don't disappoint me!"

Bluster stood under the bananatransporter. As he was saying, "And be sure to study, Stilton! I will be **test** —"

HE COMPLETELY DISAPPEARED.

Just as Bluster dematerialized, Beaker's hologram appeared — and the artifacts were in his paw! Bluster had already arrived!

Beaker said, "Geronimo, thank you for these

pistachiacious artifacts! We really didn't expect the second one, and **Professor Sandsnout** is very excited — it's perfect for the mouseum!"

Everyone on the Bananacraft cheered. "Hooray!"

"Now, there are still two artifacts we need," Beaker continued, "and time is running out. You only have **twenty-eight hours** to get back here."

I looked at my wristwatch in surprise. "Twenty hours have already passed?! That's impossible!"

Twenty hours have already passed?!

Beaker replied, "Regular watches don't work on the Bananacraft!" Then he bit into a piece of pistachio cake and started squeaking with his mouth full. "Exffuse me, I

156

Chomp! Chomp!

waff hungrfy . . . pluff it's pifstachio . . . Mmm! *Chomp, chomp.* It would bfe smarf to geff a MOVFE ON! *Chomp, chomp.* I can do iff from here wiff a fuper fpecial banana booft! Ready?

"GOOOOOOO!"

The machine started, and we were tossed around like marbles for what seemed to me (and my poor stomach) like an endless amount of time. Finally, the Bananacraft hit the ground and stopped with a jolt.

KATHUNK!

Trap stood up and went to have a look at the bananatimer: it said 1579.

He yelled, "All hands on deck, the CARIBBEAN SEA awaits! Sun, palm trees, fresh fruit juice, hammocks, relaxatioooon: I can

already tell this is the life for me! Yo, ho, ho!

"AND NOW . . .

TO THE

BANANATRANSPORTER!"

FRANCIS DRAKE'S PIRATES

AND YOU, WHAT CAN YOU DO, RAT?!

We found ourselves on a dock, surrounded by a GROUP OF PIRATES. They didn't look very friendly!

The mouse who seemed to be the captain approached me and looked me up and down. He had a *bandana* tied on his head and was wearing a pair of *pants* that only went to his knees, a leather belt, and a dirty, flea-ridden shirt that clearly hadn't been washed in who knows how many days — or months — or years.

The pirate looked at me threateningly and said, "Salivating sharks! Where did you pop out from, you rats?"

And like an echo, I heard another voice **CAW**, "Rats . . . rats . . ."

Strange! Who had said that?

I stuttered fearfully, "M-my name is Gerry . . . Gerry Stilton."

"Stilton, huh?" the pirate said, raising an **EYEBROW**. "So you aren't Spanish?"

Once again, before I could respond, I heard, "Spanish . . . Spanish . . ."

Salivating sharks! Where did you pop out from?

My name is . . . Gerry Stilton!

A BIT OF HISTORY ABOUT PIRATES

A pirate is someone who attacks and robs a ship at sea. (The word comes from the Greek *peiratēs*, which comes from the word *peiran*, meaning "to attempt.") Piracy has occurred throughout history, even as far back as 1400 BC on the Mediterranean Sea! The "golden age" of piracy occurred in the Caribbean Sea and surrounding areas in the seventeenth and eighteenth centuries, when France and England hired many privateers to ransack Spanish ships.

PRIVATEERS AND BUCCANEERS

PRIVATEERS were pirates with official papers called letters of marque. They were private individuals hired by a government to attack and rob ships and cities belonging to a rival country. They made money by keeping part of the booty they stole, and they often attacked ships they had not been asked to attack.

BUCCANEERS originally lived on Hispaniola (an island made up of Haiti and the Dominican Republic), which was owned by Spain. The buccaneers were French and hunted meat that they smoked on grills (their name comes from the French word *boucanier*, which is a grill), and they also began raiding Spanish ships.

PIRATE TIDBITS

PARROTS: Pirates who sailed through the tropics often brought exotic birds and animals home to Europe from their trips as souvenirs and to sell. Parrots were particularly desirable because of their magnificent colors and intelligence.

APPEARANCE: Their faces and arms were often tanned and weathered from the wind and sun.

WALK: On land, pirates often walked with a wide stance and swayed as they moved because of the many months they spent on the swaying decks of their ships.

CLOTHING: Pirates dressed in the same kind of practical clothing that any sailor of the time would have, though they were often depicted in fancier clothing by illustrators who never saw them!

AGE: Pirates were often in their twenties, because they were old enough to work but young enough to withstand the exhausting sea life.

The Caribbean in the sixteenth century

Strange! Who had said that?

I shook my snout quickly and responded, "Oh no, sir, I am not."

He lowered his gaze and pointed his super-long **pawnail**. "And that? Is that yours, rat?"

I looked where he was pointing and turned as **pale** as mozzarella. The miniaturized **Bananacraft** was on  the ground! Trap leaped over to pick it up, saying, "Whoops! Excuse me, dear sirs, but this is mine! Tools of the trade — I am a **CHEF**, and this is my ingredient, ready to be cooked and eaten! Indeed, I'm a fabumouse chef!"

A voice cawed, "Chef! Chef! He said chef! Chef!"

Strange! Who had said that?

Only then did I notice that, perched on the pirate's shoulder, there was a . . . **PARROT**!

Trap performed a little song and dance. *"If you want to eat it all, I'm the only one to call! For Trap is my name and cooking is my game. Appetizers, soups, and any kind of slop, I will feed you till you drop!"*

The **PIRATE** seemed very interested in my cousin's words. Then he turned to me once more. "So your friend is a chef, and I guess those are his helpers," he said, pointing to Benjamin, Trappy, and Creepella. Then he said to me, threateningly, "And you? What can you do, rat?"

The rascally **PARROT** repeated, "Rat! Rat! He's a dirty rat!" and **FLEW** around, cawing it over and over.

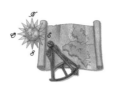

STILTON THE CARPENTER

What could I say? I needed an idea. Luckily, Trappy whispered, "G, leave this to me: I know a ton about **PIRATES** and what they need on their ships." She cleared her throat and squeaked aloud, "He is a great expert in **CARPENTRY**!"

The pirate's eyes widened. "Catfish whiskers! You're just what we need!" he said. "My name is Sullivan, and the parrot here is **Mr. Jones**."

"Ha, ha, ha! Mr. Jones! What a formal name for a parrot!" I joked, chucking.

But Sullivan didn't seem to share my humor.

Mr. Jones cawed, "That rat gets on my nerves."

The pirate cracked his knuckles and said, "Mine, too . . . He just might need to learn a LESSON."

ROLES ABOARD A PIRATE SHIP

CAPTAIN: A captain was elected by the pirate crew, and other than in battle, his authority could be overruled by a majority vote of the crew. A captain needed to be bold and decisive in battle, but even-tempered to unite the crew.

QUARTERMASTER: Also elected by the crew, he oversaw day-to-day operations, settled disputes on board, and was in charge of dividing up any loot the pirates stole.

BOATSWAIN: This petty officer was responsible for the keeping the sails, ropes, and ship in general in good shape for travel and battle.

CARPENTER: This professional was very important — he maintained and repaired all the wooden parts of the ship. Since pirates were outlaws, they couldn't dock at ports to fix their ships, so it was essential to have a carpenter on board!

COOK: He made the food for everyone! Often this role was just assigned to one of the crew mice.

RULES ON THIS SHIP

- Everyone has the right to vote and to share any fresh provisions.
- Candles must be blown out at 8:00 p.m.
- Always be ready for attacks.
- Women and children cannot come aboard.
- Those who desert combat will be punished by abandonment at sea!

The other pirates gathered around us, looking threatening. Shiver me Swiss cheese! I began to sweat.

Trap whispered to me, "Geronimo, you're a DISASTER at jokes. Leave this to me. I'm an expert!"

Then Trap cleared his throat and said, "Hey there, mice! Let's all relax a bit and have a few laughs!"

Let's have a few laughs!

He told some jokes, and they were a mouserific hit! The pirate mice were rolling on the ground, clutching their bellies in laughter.

Trap chuckled and said to Creepella, *"I may not be a knight so grand, but at jokes, I am the best in the land!"*

Everyone recovered from the jokes, and

Q: How did the young mouse afford to buy his pirate ship?
A: He got it on *sail*!

Q: What did the ocean say to the pirate mouse?
A: Nothing — it just *waved*.

Q: Why does it take so long for pirates to learn the alphabet?
A: Because they spend years at *C*!

Q: What's orange and sounds like a parrot?
A: A carrot!

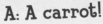

JOKES!

Q: What's a pirate's least
favorite vegetable?
A: *Leeks!*

Q: Why do seagulls fly over the sea?
A: Because if they flew over
the bay, they'd be *bagels!*

Q: Why couldn't the mouse play
cards with the pirate?
A: Because he was
standing on the deck!

Q: Why did the pirate get
an A in debate class?
A: Because he loved
to *ARR*-gue!

Sullivan said, "Come on, we'll introduce you to our **CAPTAIN**, and then we'll be ready to set sail."

"I thought you were the captain!" Trappy said.

Sullivan shook his snout. "No, not me! I'm the quartermaster." He led us to an inn, and as he opened the door, he said, "He is the captain . . . *Francis Drake*! Hey, Captain, I found, you some cooks and a carpenter!"

RAT-MUNCHING RATTLESNAKES!
SIR FRANCIS DRAKE?!

Just hearing his name made my whiskers tremble in fright! I'd already met him on another *Journey Through Time**!

Benjamin saw that I was trembling and reassured me. "Don't be afraid, Uncle G! Unlike Cleopatra, Francis Drake can't remember us.

---

* Dear rodent readers, do you remember? We met in *Lost in Time: The Fourth Journey Through Time*!

When we met him before, it was 1595 — now it's 1579, which is sixteen years earlier. Francis Drake can't know who we are, because he hasn't met us yet!"

Cheese niblets! My nephew was right.

Thank goodmouse!

Sir Francis Drake

(Devonshire, England, c. 1540–43, at sea near Panama, January 28, 1596)

He was a privateer, a sea captain, mayor of an English city, and a naval officer. From 1577 to 1580, he sailed all the way around the globe, and on his return, he was knighted by Queen Elizabeth I herself. In 1587, he helped delay for a year the invasion of England by the Spanish Armada.

MY FAVORITE PIRAAAAATE!

Trappy **threw** herself inside the inn and scurried over to Francis Drake. Then she shouted like a superfan,

"You're my favorite pirate!"

A bit annoyed, he clarified, "I am not a pirate. I'm a privateer who works in the name of *Queen Elizabeth!*"

The other patrons in the inn stood up and squeaked together, "Long live the queen!"

Francis Drake, who was much younger than when we had met him before, looked at us suspiciously. "You fish snouts! Do you not exalt our leader?!"

Great Gorgonzola! It was best not to make him mad.

"Long live the queen!" we all squeaked at once.

Then Trappy continued. "Anyway, as I was saying, you are my favorite pira . . . I mean, my favorite privateer! I know everything about you! I mean *everything*! For example —"

I rushed over and **covered** Trappy's snout, whispering, "Trappy, remember that we come

from the **FUTURE**! If we say too much, we could seem like Spanish spies!"

She nodded and gave me a thumbs-up. Then she turned back to Francis Drake and held out a piece of paper.

"Captain Drake, can I have an autograph? Pretty please, with cheese on top?"

Then she pawed him a feather pen and some ink.

181

Francis Drake sighed, but he took the pen. With a flourish of his PAW, he gave Trappy an autograph.

Then the privateer said, "Well, it's time to set sail. There are ships to plunder, loot to steal, jewels to snatch, and most importantly . . . battles to fight!"

"B-b-battles?!" I stammered. "Whaaat?

There must be some mistake. I'm a peaceful rat!"

Francis Drake gave me a **thump** on the back so powerful it almost knocked me over and said, "Come on, you scurvy squid! Don't be a *coward*!"

We left the inn and reached the port's pier, where there were a few **dinghies** tied up. We boarded one and rowed to an inlet.

Captain Drake looked satisfied as he announced, "There it is! Introducing my most precious jewel!"

ANCHORS AWEIGH!

We boarded the **Golden Hind**, Francis Drake's galleon. The wooden planks creaked with every pawstep. There was much confusion on board. Tarred ropes were tossed onto the deck along with **moldy sails**, barrels, and baskets. Cheese and crackers, these pirates sure weren't tidy! But each mouse was busy doing something: **rolling up** ropes, tying on sails, cleaning the deck.

Heave-ho!

That's good!

Argh!

Anchors aweigh!

Soon I heard Drake's voice yelling, "LIFT THE SAILS, CREW! ANCHORS AWEIGH!"

The sails filled with wind, and the *Golden Hind* was off, moving slowly at first, and then more and more quickly. Captain Drake helmed the ship, and we all enjoyed the *breeze* off the Caribbean Sea. I closed my eyes and exclaimed, "**Ahhh!** What a fabumouse breeze!"

Then a voice behind us thundered, "Crusty clams! What are you doing here on deck?!"

Get to work!

How beautiful!

Answer: Sixteen fins

It was Sullivan, with Mr. Jones on his shoulder (of course).

He continued. "We didn't bring you aboard so you could lounge around, you lazyfurs! Get in the **Galley** and get dinner ready! And get to work, carpenter!"

Mr. Jones cawed, "Lazyfurs! Lazyfurs!"

Sullivan kept squeaking. "And let me be clear: we don't want our usual slop for dinner. When we set sail, we usually celebrate until late and eat a feast. So we want a whisker-licking good meal, do you hear me?!"

Mr. Jones flapped his wings. "Hear me?! Hear me?!"

"Otherwise we'll feed you to the **sharks**, got it?!" Sullivan concluded, pointing to the **plank** that jutted out over the sea.

TERMS TO KNOW ON A PIRATE SHIP

BELOWDECKS: the part of the ship beneath the main deck

BOW: the front of the ship

BRIDGE: a room or platform on the deck from which the captain commands the ship

CAREEN: to ground a ship on its side in order to clean or repair the hull

CAST OFF: to untie the boat so it can leave the dock

DECK: the highest level of the ship, which is partially or totally uncovered

GALLEY: the ship's kitchen and where the pantry is; located belowdecks

HELM: the wheel that allows you to steer a ship

HULL: the shell of the ship, part of which goes underwater

LINE: a rope used on a ship

MAST: a long pole that rises from the deck and supports the sails

PORT: the left side of the ship when facing the bow

SHROUD: the collection of lines that make up part of the fixed rigging that keeps the mast stable

STARBOARD: the right side of the ship when facing the bow

STERN: the back of the ship

WHAT DID YOU SAY YOUR NAME WAS?!

Trap called our time-traveling group together. "Okay, I have a plan," he said. Then he turned to Creepella and bragged, "Have I told you that I'm basically a walking cookbook? I'm a real master chef! I even won the reality show *MousterChef*! You'll always eat well when you are with me!"

I won the reality show MousterChef!

As we went belowdecks, Trap kept squeaking. "We'll cook a first-class meal. I have a thousand recipes in mind! These pirates will be so full, they won't be able to get up from the table. They'll repay us with a sack full of gold coins, which we can bring back as an artifact. And I'm sure no one would care if we took a handful for ourselves — the mouseum wouldn't mind having fewer coins, right, Ger — "

He didn't finish his thought, because he BASHED his head hard on the galley doorframe and ended up sprawled on the ground.

Bonk!

"Oh no! Are you okay?" Trappy squeaked.

We gathered around him. He was knocked out, and there was already an enormouse **bump** on his forehead!

Finally, Trap came to. He had a smile across his snout, but it seemed like he wasn't totally with it.

I was worried. "Trap, do you feel all right?"

He smiled. "What was that, my dear?"

"How are you? Does your head hurt?" I asked.

He sat up. "Ah, my head? Well, yes, it hurts a bit . . . What happened? Where are we?"

Trappy took his paw. "What do you mean 'where are we'?" she asked. "We're on Francis Drake's SHIP! Don't you remember?"

Trap smiled. "Ah right, the ship! So . . . we're

back at the amousement park?"

I took a closer look at his snout. He seemed pretty confused. I repeated, "Trap, are you all right?"

He patted me on the back. "Of course, dear mouse! What did you say your name was?!"

Uh-oh. I turned toward my friends and said, "I think that bonk on the head caused Trap to forget everything! Hopefully he'll recover soon, but for now, he can't be our chef. And the pirates are expecting a food mousterpiece!"

Rancid ricotta, WE WERE IN ENORMOUSE TROUBLE!

SAVE US, BANANAPHONE!

We looked at one another, worried. Without my cousin's recipes, how would we manage to not become SHARK FOOD?!

You mice will be mashed!

As if that wasn't bad enough, Mr. Jones arrived and began to fly around the galley, cawing, "You mice will be mashed! Squashed! Pulverized!"

Yuck!

He did a few loops in the air, and on his way out, left me a little PRESENT on my head. Eww!

Benjamin LIT up and said, "Of course! The Bananacraft!

Remember? When it's miniaturized, it becomes a **bananaphone**! We can communicate with present-day New Mouse City to get some delicious recipes."

"We could ask *Mama Gina*, Bluster's mom!" I exclaimed. "She is a marvemouse cook!"

Trap was already **DROOLING**. "Did you say pizza? I would gobble down a **four-cheese** pizza faster than the mouse ran up the clock!"

MAMA GINA

Mama Gina is Bluster's mom. She is a fabumouse cook and specializes in pizzas. The recipe for her most famous pizza, Mama Gina's Pie, is a secret!

Hello, Beaker?

Trappy **exclaimed**, "Save us, bananaphone!"

Benjamin got in contact with Beaker. Luckily, Bluster was there, too, and he had Mama Gina's **Big Book of Recipes**!

Beaker read aloud the ingredients and recipes to make appetizers, a first course, a second course, and dessert.

Trappy proved herself to be an excellent **team leader**: she gave us each a **JOB** to do.

"Creepella will make the cheese and veggie appetizers, Benjamin

Here's a good recipe!

Buried treasure omelets!

and I will make the buccaneer's beef jerky and the buried treasure omelets, and Uncle G will prepare the cheesecake!"

Trap watched our preparations silently, then complained, "Don't we get to eat at this amousement park?! I'm hungry!"

MENU

AHOY! AN APPETIZER!
Vegetables and cheese

BUCCANEER'S BEEF JERKY
Extra spicy (for strong palates)

BURIED TREASURE OMELETS
(filled with cheese and potatoes)

And for dessert . . .
CORSAIR CHEESECAKE

Creepella approached me and said, "My darling rat, all this cooking has gotten me thinking. What kinds of food do you think are best for a wedding?"

I was trying to concentrate and measure the sugar for the batter, but I had to respond. "I'm not really sure. I've never thought about it before."

"Oh, that can't be true," she said, smiling. Then she frowned. "I bet my dad would love to cook for my wedding!"

"Are you sure? All he does is tell jokes from morning to night!" I said.

Creepella sighed. "That's true, he does love his jokes."

How can you spot a chilly ghost?
Instead of wearing a sheet, he's wearing a wool blanket!

Boris von Cacklefur, Creepella's dad

"The last time I saw him, he challenged me to a duel . . . of jokes!"

She shrugged. "It's what he is good at!"

"That's enough chatter, you two!" Trappy called. "We don't have much time!"

I shook my snout and grabbed one of the CONTAINERS that was in front of me to measure out what looked like sugar.

We cooked for about three hours. At last, our pirate feast was ready! And it was all thanks to Benjamin and Trappy!

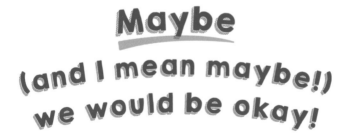

Maybe

(and I mean maybe!)
we would be okay!

BLECH!

We left the galley single file and went to the dining room, where there was an enormouse table of **starving pirates** waiting for us. Francis Drake was at the head of the table.

With a fork in his paw, Sullivan said, "It's about time, you slimy clownfish! I hope that this dinner is worth the wait!"

We didn't even manage to put the trays on the table before the pirates grabbed all the food.

"**Time to eat!**" they all squeaked, and dove their snouts into their plates.

The appetizers were gobbled up in the blink of an eye. So was the meat, despite being super spicy. (Mama Gina loves putting HOT PEPPER FLAKES in her recipes!)

When we brought out the omelets, the pace of

eating had slowed a bit, and when we served the
dessert, the pirates' bellies were already nice
and full.

Captain Drake, who was quite a glutton,
proclaimed, "**STOP, CREW!** I will taste
this delicious-looking dessert first. Tell me: who
made this?"

I lifted my paw shyly.

Drake gave me harsh look. **Gulp!** I knew
quite well that he was a surly mouse who had a
temper.

If it's not good, all
the worse for you!

He thundered, "If this
dessert isn't delicious, it will
be all the worse for you,
fishbrain . . . But if I like
it, I'll reward you with
gold coins, Stilton!"

Then he tasted the
cheesecake.

As he chewed, I felt satisfied. Thanks to my contribution, we would be repaid with **gold coins**, and we could leave on the Bananacraft!

Drake swallowed, and . . .

Let's see here . . .

"**Blech!**"

He had a disgusted expression on his snout! He turned toward me and shouted furiously, "Grab that rat! Get all of them! I want them crushed — pulverized — fed to the sharks!"

"B-but what did I d-do?!" I stammered.

Blech!

Why, why, why does everything always happen to me?

209

Had I not followed the recipe as well as I'd thought? I scooped a bit of cheesecake on my finger, and . . . blech, blech, blech!

Holey cheese! The cake was SALTY!

No wonder Drake was so disgusted. I'd gotten distracted, and had mistaken the salt for sugar!

Feed them to the sharks!

What a nice parrot!

The pirates captured us and tied us up in a flash.

Mr. Jones cawed and cawed. "Feed them to the sharks! To the sharks!"

We were done for!

I climbed onto the plank, and Sullivan poked my tail with a **DaGGer**. "So, rat: will you jump on your own, or do you need a push?"

A SUPER-SUPER-SECRET MAP

Suddenly, I heard Trappy's voice yelling, "Wait! If you let us go, we'll give you a **super-super-secret** map to a **super-super-secret** treasure! Guaranteed gold for everyone! I swear on my whiskers!"

Trappy understood that *gold* was the magic word to get the attention of those **CREEPS**. In fact, Francis Drake immediately stopped Sullivan from continuing to poke me.

Heeeelp!

Ha, ha, ha!

Chomp!

"Let him go!"

Sullivan huffed. "Oh, all right!"

What a relief!

But when Sullivan jumped down off the plank, it bounced down, and as if from a catapult, I was **TOSSED** in the air.

"HEEEEEEEELP!"

I yelled at the top of my lungs. "I'm too fond of my fur!"

I closed my eyes, waiting for my unlucky end. But someone grabbed me midair, and I landed on the ship's deck.

I WAS SAFE AND SOUND!

Then Drake ordered, "Untie the prisoners!"

I must admit, even if he was a privateer, Francis Drake was a brave rodent. Do you want to know what had happened?

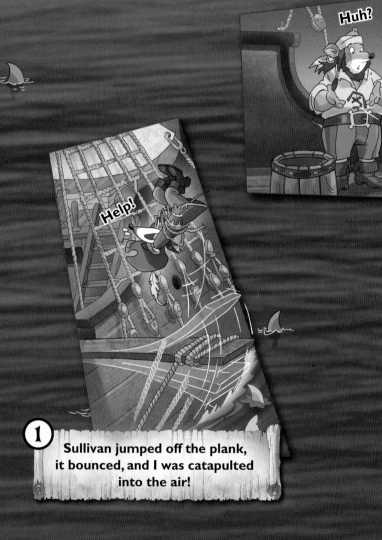

1

Sullivan jumped off the plank, it bounced, and I was catapulted into the air!

Give me that!
2
Drake grabbed Sullivan's sword, swung it hard, and cut a line tied to the ship's mast!
3
Then he grabbed on to the rope as it launched upward . . .
Got him!
I'm saved!
4
And he grabbed me in midair! Phew . . . I got lucky on that one!

Where did I put it?

Drake turned to Trappy. "So? Where is this map?

Cold sweat started trickling down my fur. What was Trappy's plan? We didn't have any map! But she seemed calm, and **WINKED** at me.

She rummaged into her pockets, and gave Captain Drake a **map** that I recognized at once: it was a map of the amousement park!

Is this the map?

Here it is!

Great Gorgonzola! What a good idea! It was **RISKY**, though . . . If the pirates discovered our trick, we would be fed to the sharks. **Squeeeeak!**

Francis Drake looked at the map carefully. "Hmm . . . interesting!"

Then he turned to the crew, satisfied, and proclaimed, "Privateers, prepare yourselves: our next adventure is in search of treasure! Tomorrow we will raise the anchor and head

toward the island of TORTUGA! Hip, hip . . ."

The crew all responded together, "Hooray! Hooray! Hooray!"

Then Drake took a **bag** full of jingling coins

and gave it to Trappy. "Here you go — this is an advance. If we really find the **treasure**, you'll get your share of the loot. Privateers always divvy up everything. **It's the rule!**"

Then he concluded, "But if we *don't* find the treasure, you squidheads will be dinner for the sharks!"

Trappy took the bag and opened it. There were **gold coins** inside!

Thank goodmouse! Not only were we saved, we also had an **ARTIFACT** from the 1500s to bring to the mouseum!

It's Time to
Dive in the Sea

Night fell, and the whole crew went to sleep. Captain Drake was in his cabin, but the other pirates snoozed on the **DECK**.

We were leaning against a barrel, pretending to rest. But really, we were waiting for the right moment to leave the *Golden Hind*!

Finally, all the pirates were *SNORING*. (And I mean *all* of them! What a racket!)

Trappy whispered, "We need to get out of here before they figure out that the map is **FAKE**."

"We passed a small island not long ago," Benjamin whispered. "If we can get to it, we can enlarge the Bananacraft and dematerialize."

"But how will we manage to reach it?" I asked, starting to panic. "There are pirates sleeping on the lifeboats, and the sea is full of **SHARKS**!"

Trappy smiled and said, "Let's stay calm. I saw something in the **galley** that will help us. Come on!"

We went down belowdecks and found some

How will we reach the island?

Well?

I saw something that will help us!

ENORMOUSE BARRELS. They were really heavy, but we managed to get ourselves into them and into the water, then paddled with ladles until we reached land.

On the beach, Trap tripped as he was getting out of his barrel, and **bonked** his head on the side as he fell to the ground.

"Ouch! What a blow!" he squeaked.

I feel like this is your fault!

Welcome back, Cousin!

"Trap, are you okay?" Creepella asked.

"Oof! My HEAD is killing me!" Trap said. "What happened? Geroni*moomoo*, I feel like this is your fault . . ." Then he looked at me more closely and exclaimed, in his usual tone, "Did you know you have a PIMPLE on your snout?"

I jumped up to hug him and happily cried, "Welcome back, Cousin!"

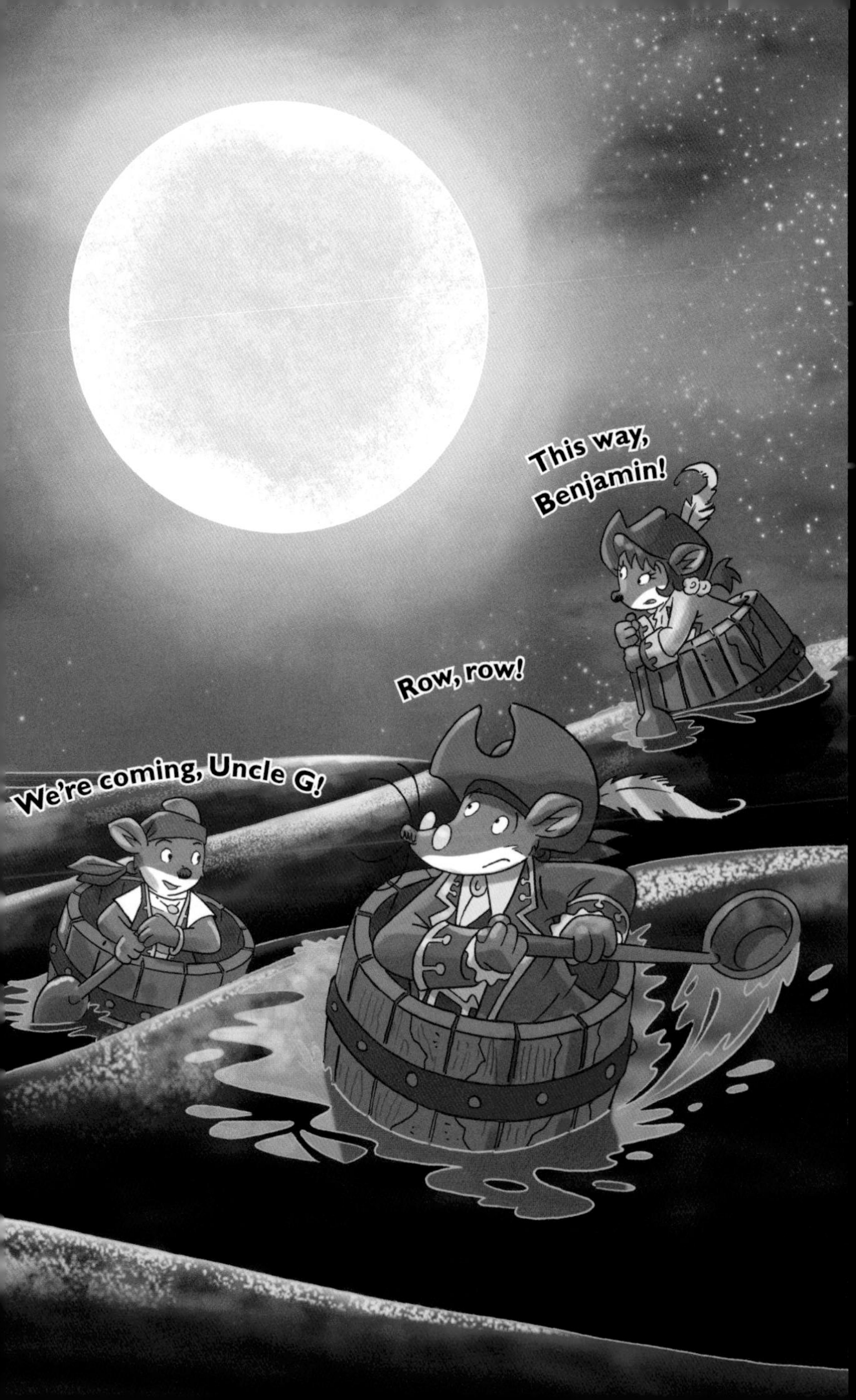
This way, Benjamin!
Row, row!
We're coming, Uncle G!

TEN HOURS AND COUNTING!

We got aboard the Bananacraft. Once we were all settled, we looked at the **bananatimer**:

There was no time to lose! We put the bag of gold coins in the **bananatransporter** and sent it directly to present-day New Mouse City.

A few seconds later, a *HOLOGRAM* of Beaker Poirat appeared to talk to us.

"Time travelers, you found an artifact from the 1500s! Now the only one missing is from the

1700s: you'll go see Mozart. But before that, there is someone here who wants to talk to you . . ."

Next to Beaker, the entire von Cacklefur family appeared!

Creepella exclaimed, "My gloomy family! I'm so happy to see you!"

Boris von Cacklefur was the first to speak. "So, my dear daughter, are you enjoying this vacation through time?"

I tried to interrupt. "Well, actually, it's not a —"

Boris continued. "I hope Geronimo is showing you a good time."

"A good time?!" I repeated.

Boris nodded. "Snakes, pirates, there is no way you aren't having loads of fun!"

Creepella clapped her paws in excitement. "You would not believe the fun we are having! I wish you could all be here."

I couldn't even manage to respond.

Luckily, Beaker intervened. "Um, I'm sorry to interrupt this little moment of JOY, but time is running out. You need to leave!"

Benjamin asked, "Professor, could you give us a banana boost and make the machine go faster?"

"Let me do a few CALCULATIONS . . ." Beaker said, then nodded. "Yes! But it needs something really strong, like . . . a superpowerful bananazoid. We will charge it up with extra **banana peels**! I'll handle it!"

Beaker and the entire von Cacklefur family disappeared, and suddenly, we heard the bananatransporter sizzling.

Bzzzzzzz!

We all held our breath until we could make out the shape of . . . **Beaker Poirat**! It was really him, in the fur and whiskers!

He had with him some sort of book and . . . **a bin full of bananas**!

"Here you go, Stilton, these bananas are for you!" he exclaimed. "Of course, they aren't as good as **PISTACHIOS**, but my cousin Hercule told me that you love them, too, so it won't be a big deal for you to eat them **ALL** in the name of science!"

I started to protest. "Well, actually, I —"

But Trap was already pawing me a banana he'd

started to **PEEL**. "Geronimo, don't complain! The professor said it: it's for the ᏀᎾᎾᎠ ᎾᎦ ᎦᏟᎬᏁᏟᎬ."

I sighed, and began to stuff myself with bananas. One banana, two bananas, three bananas, four bananas, five bananas, six bananas, seven bananas, eight bananas, nine bananas, ten bananas, eleven bananas, twelve bananas, thirteen bananas, fourteen bananas, fifteen bananas, sixteen bananas, seventeen bananas, eighteen bananas, nineteen bananas, twenty bananas, twenty-one bananas, twenty-two bananas, twenty-three bananas . . . and eventually . . .

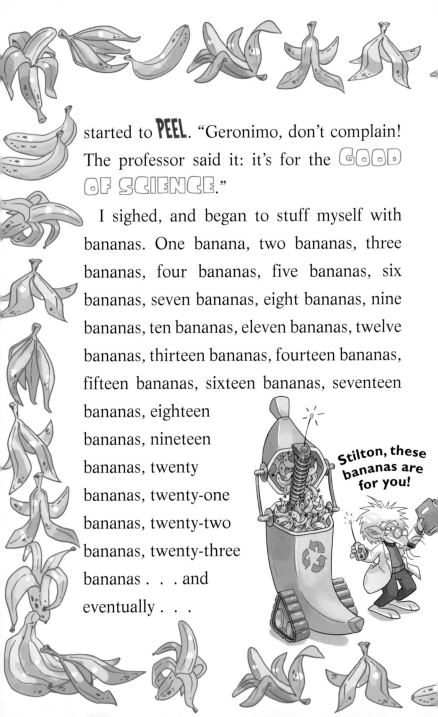

Stilton, these bananas are for you!

FIFTY BANANAS! OOF!

Finally, we had all the peels we needed for the banana boost.

As Beaker picked up the last peel, he said, "Well done, Geronimo! That's fifty bananas: *A RECORD*!"

Trap shrugged. "He was just doing his job."

I couldn't get up. All I could do was ask, "Does anyone have some ginger ale?"

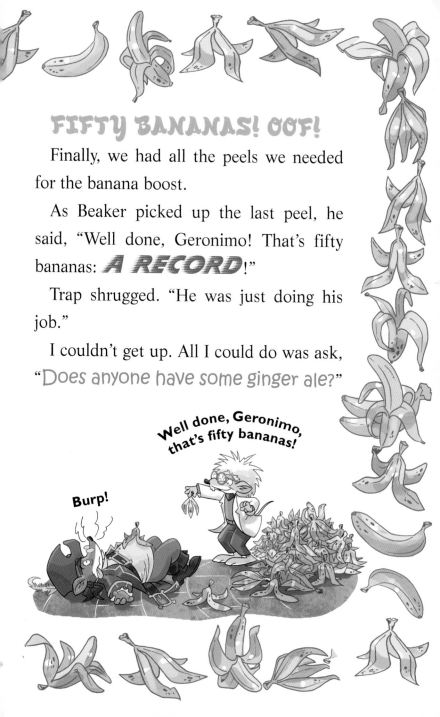

Well done, Geronimo, that's fifty bananas!

Burp!

WE WANT TO MEET A CHILD PRODIGY!

Beaker approached the bananatimer and began to input the settings. "Okay, so, to visit Mozart, we could go to the time he was composing his —"

"Wait a minute, Professor Poirat!" Trappy and Benjamin interrupted.

Benjamin continued. "We want to see Mozart when he was still a young mouseling. We heard that he was called a child prodigy!"

I smiled. "I think that's a fabumouse idea! Often young mice have things to teach us adults!"

"So it's decided." Beaker smiled. "I also brought a book with the **scores*** of the greatest composers in history, including Mozart!"

Trap took the **BOOK** and flipped through it

* A score is a complete copy of a musical composition.

arrogantly. "Any mouse could write these! I'm **great** at composing — listen here: *Traveling through time is always fun, until we have to turn and run.* There's one more artifact to find, but I can do it — I've made up my mind!"

I was going to reply, but Beaker started the **banana boost** and . . .

Banana boost in action!

MOZART IN THE COURT OF VIENNA

MY HEAD ITCHES!

We found ourselves on a street in Salzburg, Austria, the city where Wolfgang Amadeus Mozart was born in 1756. My head immediately felt itchy. I put my paw up to scratch it and realized that I was wearing a wig — and so were my travel companions! How uncomfortable!

Trap was SCRATCHING his fur under the wig.

"We'll have to deal with the wigs — in this time, it was in style for *everyone* to wear them!" Creepella exclaimed.

I suddenly remembered one of Bluster's old lessons and said, "That's right! Also, you should know that . . ."

Fashion in the 1700s

The fashion of this period is defined as "rococo," which was an artistic style characterized by elegance and elaborate, ornate decoration. The word comes from the French word *rocaille*, which describes the shells and rocks used in gardens as embellishments.

Women's Fashion

Women wore splendid gowns with plenty of frills and trim, and large, elaborate hairstyles and wigs. *Pannier* (frames made out of wicker) were worn underneath the skirts on the hips to make them stick out at the sides. They could be up to eighteen feet wide!

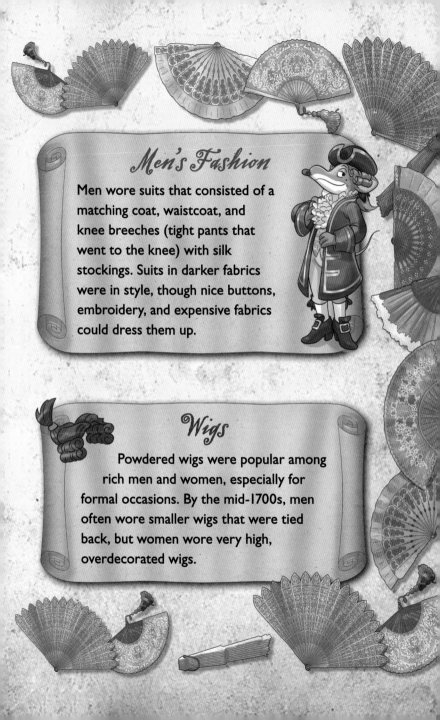

Men's Fashion

Men wore suits that consisted of a matching coat, waistcoat, and knee breeches (tight pants that went to the knee) with silk stockings. Suits in darker fabrics were in style, though nice buttons, embroidery, and expensive fabrics could dress them up.

Wigs

Powdered wigs were popular among rich men and women, especially for formal occasions. By the mid-1700s, men often wore smaller wigs that were tied back, but women wore very high, overdecorated wigs.

"Well, you do know a thing or two!" Beaker said, impressed. "I didn't expect that: Bluster told me that you were a **terrible student**!"

I sighed. Convincing Bluster Squeak of my intelligence was an impossible mission!

At that moment, we heard voices behind us: there was a **ratlet** of about seven years old being accompanied by what I assumed were his older sister and father. The mouse approached us and said, "Hello, my name is Leopold Mozart. Are you the mice who are to take us to Passau by carriage and then to Vienna by boat?"

Holey cheese! It was Wolfgang Amadeus Mozart and his family!

Trap jumped in with a response. "Of course! I am obviously the leader of the group," he said, then took his wig off like it was a hat and bowed. "We are the Stiltonschultz Family, at your service!"

I WHiSPeReD, "What are you saying?! We don't know anything about carriage transport, let alone boat transport!"

Trap shushed me. "Shhh . . . minor details. Now load the luggage onto the carriage!"

Are you the mice who will take us?

MY NAME IS WOLFGANG AMADEUS MOZART

Unfortunately, that meant I had to load Mozart's enormouse harpsichord onto the 𝕮𝕒𝕣𝕣𝕚𝕒𝕘𝕖. And after that, I also had to load:

eight trunks

three violins

seventeen books

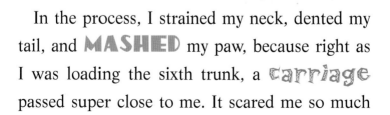

In the process, I strained my neck, dented my tail, and **MASHED** my paw, because right as I was loading the sixth trunk, a 𝕮𝕒𝕣𝕣𝕚𝕒𝕘𝕖 passed super close to me. It scared me so much that I jumped, lost my balance, and dropped the trunk! Luckily, it just barely missed totally **CRUSHING** my paw.

Moldy mozzarella! How stressful!

Finally, we all boarded the carriage. Trap and Beaker went up to the box (which is where the

As I was loading the sixth trunk, a carriage passed super close to me . . .

driver usually sits), and Creepella, Benjamin, Trappy, Mozart's family, and I sat inside.

Little Wolfgang looked at Benjamin and Trappy CURIOUSLY, and then he smiled at them and said, "My name is Wolfgang Amadeus, and this is my sister, Nannerl. And you?"

Argh!

Phew . . . missed me by a whisker!

I jumped, and the trunk nearly crushed my paw!

Trappy responded, "Hi! I am Trappy and this is Benjamaus. What are you going to do in **Vienna**?"

Wolfgang shrugged and answered, "We need to **PLAY** in someone's court — I don't remember . . ."

His father, Leopold, frowned and said severely, "To the court of *Empress Maria Theresa*, Wolferl*! It isn't just *someone*! And she wants you to play, because you are a child prodigy."

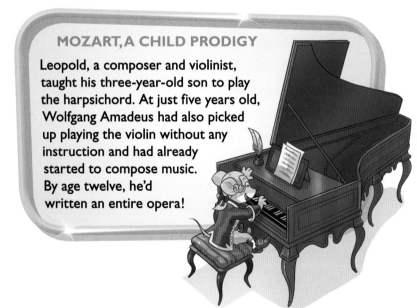

MOZART, A CHILD PRODIGY

Leopold, a composer and violinist, taught his three-year-old son to play the harpsichord. At just five years old, Wolfgang Amadeus had also picked up playing the violin without any instruction and had already started to compose music. By age twelve, he'd written an entire opera!

* Wolferl was the nickname that Wolfgang's father called him.

Trappy noticed that Wolfgang's sister was off to the side, silent. She asked, "Do you play, too, Nannerl?"

Nannerl smiled shyly. "Yes, I do! But . . . well, he is the genius!"

Hearing that, Wolfgang hugged her and said, "Big sister, you are **amazing**! And I love you very much!"

NANNERL

Nannerl, which is a nickname for "Marie Anna," was a highly talented harpsichord and piano player (and may also have been a composer), and she accompanied her beloved brother on performance tours through Europe. But her father ended her music career when she was eighteen so that she could get married, which was typical at that time in history.

Answer: Wolfgang's father is wearing a wristwatch on his wrist. Wristwatches were only invented at the end of the nineteenth century!

"That's enough, Wolferl," Leopold said. "Did you remember to bring your **scores** for the concert at the queen's court?"

Wolfgang nodded. "Of course, Father."

How exciting — we were right there with one of the **GREATEST GENIUSES** in history!

I looked at the young Nannerl Mozart and thought about how she could have become really famouse, too, if only she had lived in a **DIFFERENT TIME** . . .

I think Trappy had the same thought, because she suddenly took Nannerl's paw and *smiled* at her.

Maybe It's Time to Take a Little Break

After a few days of traveling by carriage, we reached Passau.

"Here we are!" Trap announced. "While Geronimüller unloads the luggage, Mr. Mozart and I will go and get tickets for our boat trip."

I tried to protest. "Why me?!"

Trap whispered, "Oh shush, Geronimo, just do what I say!"

So I had to unload all the luggage. And then, once Trap and Leopold returned with the tickets, I had to load all luggage onto the boat!

Huff, huff, pant . . .
Why, why, why
did everything always happen to me?

THE TRIP ON THE DANUBE

The trip on the Danube (from Passau to Vienna) was valued by the Habsburg nobility. During the trip, the boat would hold parties with music and small concerts with famous musicians, games, and shows featuring clowns and acrobats.

Once we got onto the boat, though, I was stunned. There were so many refined gentlemice, elegant lady rats, and even ACROBATS to entertain the passengers during the trip!

I looked at my travel companions, beaming — that is, until the ship began to move. We bobbed back and forth, and waved UP and **DOWN** . . . and, as you may know, I suffer from seasickness!

The result? After a few hours on the river, I was

GREEN WITH NAUSEA.

Creepella found me and said, "My darling mouse, I was thinking . . . let's arrange for acrobats at our wedding, too!"

"What wedding?!" I asked. Gulp! I didn't want to lose my cheese!

"Oh, you silly mouse!" she responded. "My, what a lovely greenish color you are! You look fantastic!"

"F-f-fantastic?! I feel awful!"

Great chunks of cheddar — my head was **spinning**!

At one point, I heard Trappy's squeak from afar, saying, "Would a slap on the snout cure him?"

"We could make him sniff some **stinky socks**," Trap suggested. "That usually works!"

Creepella added, "What if I gave him a kiss? It would be so romantic, just like in a fairy tale!"

Trap muttered, "I don't see how that will help!"

Finally, I started feeling better . . . but when I looked up, Creepella was just a whisker away from me!

I yelled, "I'm good! I'm great! I'm fabumouse!"

Sweet cheese!

"Fabumouse?" Leopold said, looking me up and down. "Allow me to disagree. You look **quite pale**, Geronimüller!"

Beaker took out a magnifying glass and stared into my eyes. Finally he said, "Oh yes. This **greenish color**, this dizziness, this foolish nature: I think the subject is at risk of croaking! Maybe we should take a little break . . ."

"**C-c-croaking?!**" I stammered.

"Don't worry, darling," Creepella reassured me. "If that happens, my dad will take care of the **casket**! Do you want it lined with velvet, or do you prefer something simpler?"

I thought I was going to faint.

Umm . . .

My dad will take care of your casket!

My dear nephew Benjamin pointed to the sky. "It's **DARK**, and the ship will stop in Linz soon. What do you say we stay on land for the **NIGHT**?"

Trap huffed. "Gerry, you're so weak! Oh fine, we'll stop."

A short while later, we got off the boat and entered an **INN**, tired and famished.

Leopold arranged for our rooms, but before going to bed, we all scarfed some bread and cheese. We were so hungry that it seemed exquisite!

While we were eating, Trap turned to Wolfgang and said, "I can't wait to hear you perform, LITTLE GENIUS!"

Two unpleasant-looking rats at the bar turned to us, interested. One of them squeaked, "*Genius, you said?*"

Trap responded, "**GENIUS! GENIUS!** You heard right: I said genius, and I will say it again. My new friend here is a real genius! He can play, and great Gouda, can he compose! You should hear him! And lucky for him, I am his manager*!"

One of the two rats was especially interested. "He composes, huh . . . who knows how much his works are **worth**?!"

"Genius," you said?

He even composes!

* A manager of a musician is someone who deals with business side of things, such as handling finances, booking and promoting performances, and more.

Trap gave him a thumbs-up. Then he turned toward Leopold and nudged him. "Perhaps you didn't know, but in addition to being a transportation expert, I am also a great manager. And this ratlet has something worth selling, trust me!"

I whispered to Trap, "What are you saying?! You aren't a manager!"

He huffed, "Geronimo, you're so fussy! Managing will be my seventeenth job!"

WHAT A NIGHT!

As the innkeeper took us to our rooms, I saw that the two creepy rats were following us with their eyes.

Strange! I didn't feel very at ease . . .

We all went up to the second floor, where it was horribly cold. **BRRRRRRRR!**

We were going to turn into mice-icles! My teeth began to chatter noisily.

CLICK CLACK CLICK

Benjamin shivered. "Uncle G, it's so c-c-cooooold!"

"Th-th-there's no central h-h-heat
in this time," I replied.

BRRRRRR!

The mouselings were in one room, Creepella was in another, Leopold went with Beaker, and I was with Trap. The innkeeper gave us one bed warmer per room.

Trap took ours and said, "I'll stick it in the bed, Geronimo. Meanwhile, you go wash up. The BATHROOM is in the courtyard."

"In the courtyard?! It's going to be even colder down there! It's freezing out!" I squeaked. My dear mouse friends, you must know that I'm a rodent who gets **quite cold**. So I put on my coat, my scarf, my boots, and my hat, and risked freezing my tail off outside.

Brrrr, how cold!

BRRRRRRRR!

Once I got back to the room, I changed quickly into my pajamas. But the ground was freezing, and so were my paws!

BRRRRRRRR!

Then I slipped under the covers . . . but jumped out of them at once. They were freezing, too!

BRRRRRRRR!

Why, why, why does everything always happen to me?

I turned to Trap. He was already snoring! How was that possible? It was too cold!

Then I realized that Trap had only put the bed warmer on his side of the bed! I woke him up and said, "Does it seem fair that you're keeping the **warmth** all for yourself?!"

He looked at me, then rolled over and huffed. "Geronimo, you're always complaining! You're never happy. I did this for you, you know — the **cold** is good for strengthening the body!"

I stared at him, squeakless.

Trap continued, "And I'm warning you: no snoring, okay? I'm a light sleeper!"

Squeak!
Why, why, why
did everything always
happen to me?

HER MAJESTY MARIA THERESA!

The next day, we set out at dawn. I was so, so tired — I hadn't closed my eyes all night. Meanwhile, my cousin was as fresh as a ball of mozzarella.

Trap looked at me and said, "You look terrible, Geronimo. Are you okay?"

"Well, not really. I didn't sleep very much, and —"

"Huh! How strange — I slept amazingly well!"

We boarded the boat. After a few days of uneventful travel, we finally reached VIENNA!

Of course, once we arrived in the city, I again had to unload the bags, and then reload them onto a carriage that would take us to the royal palace. Sigh!

Game

Look carefully at the picture. Do you see anything that doesn't belong?

Answer: The bicycle and the streetlight didn't exist during Mozart's time.

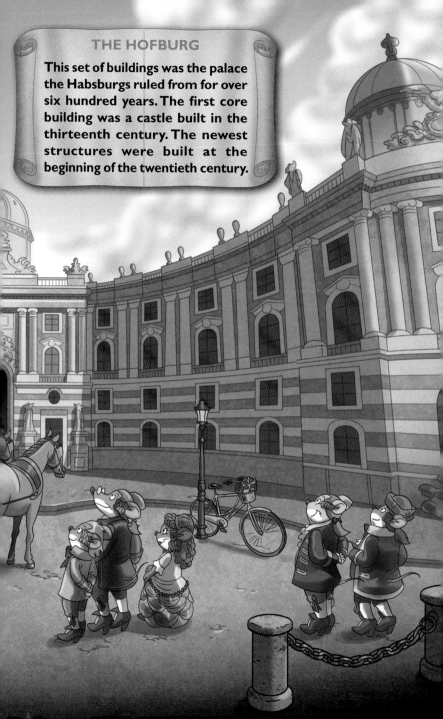

THE HOFBURG

This set of buildings was the palace the Habsburgs ruled from for over six hundred years. The first core building was a castle built in the thirteenth century. The newest structures were built at the beginning of the twentieth century.

When the palace was in sight, Leopold got so **excited**, I almost thought *he* was the one who was going to play. He said to Wolfgang, "So, are you ready? You know they are all waiting for you! First you'll **play** with Nannerl, and then you'll play the pieces you composed. You have the scores, right? You have them?"

Wolfgang smiled and responded, "Calm down, Father. The **music** is in my trunk."

My harpsichord, please!

I noticed that his behavior made him seem much **MORE ADULT** than a mouseling of his age! He was a child prodigy that was sure of his talents.

"Mr. Geronimüller," Wolfgang asked me, "could you **unload** my harpsichord and my trunk, please?"

I nodded, but just thinking about all that heavy

lifting (again!) made my back **HURT**!

As if that weren't enough, Trap began to sing at me. *"Come on now, Geronipants, he didn't ask you this by chance! Put that luggage on your back,* you big lump of cheddar Jack*! Trala here, trala there, tralalala everywhere!"*

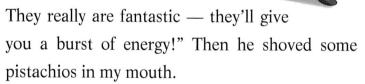

Trala here, trala there!

I loaded the trunk on my shoulders, trying not to let it fall. Beaker approached and said, "Stilton, you seem a bit tired. Why don't you try some PISTACHIOS? They really are fantastic — they'll give you a burst of energy!" Then he shoved some pistachios in my mouth.

I tried to turn my snout the other way, but with the TRUNK on my back, it was difficult. "Wait, Beaker! *Huff, puff!* Not now, I don't want any —"

But it was too late. I was forced to choke down a pawful of pistachios all at once.

Why, why, why
did everything
always happen to me?

Finally, I managed to unload the trunk and the harpsichord.

Trap said, "Good job, Geroni*maldo*! You see, when you work hard, you can get things done."

I stammered, breathless, "M-m-my name isn't Geronimaldo. It's Geronimo!"

At that moment, some **royal pages** came to meet us. "Herr Mozart, I presume?" one asked. Leopold nodded. The page continued. "Please, follow me. *Her Majesty the Queen* is waiting for you."

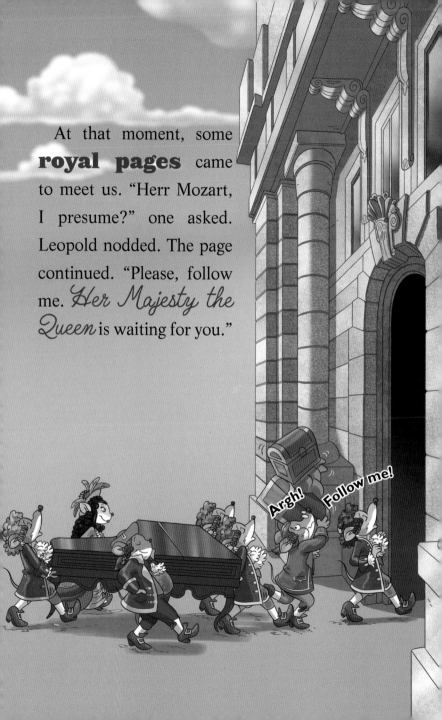

Argh!

Follow me!

I Can't Find
My Score!

We entered the **PALACE** and were struck by splendor of the rooms. There were shiny marble floors, stucco ceilings, and luxurious curtains.

Cheese niblets! What a fabumouse place!

"My little bat wing, this wouldn't be a bad spot for a wedding, either!" Creepella exclaimed.

I turned red and replied, "Who is getting married?"

"Oh, you are such a jokester!" she said, smiling.

The royal page led us to a **LARGE ROOM** and said, "You can get settled here for now and wait until I call for you. Her Majesty the Queen only wants to hear the prodigy." Then he left the room.

Wolfgang blushed and squeezed Nannerl's paw. "I'm sorry," he said.

She smiled kindly. "Don't worry, little brother: you are the **CHILD PRODIGY**. They are right."

Wolfgang protested, "But I want to play with you! You are amazing, too!"

"And we'll play soon! You'll see!" She hugged him.

Trappy huffed and whispered, "How terrible it was to be born at a time when females were seen as inferior. It's not fair!"

Creepella put a paw on her shoulder and whispered back, "You're right, little one. Luckily, things have changed through the centuries . . ."

You are the child prodigy!

Women Throughout History

1 ❋ PREHISTORY ❋

Recent studies suggest that, in prehistoric hunter-gatherer societies, males and females were actually quite equal — until farming became common practice.

2 ❋ ANCIENT EGYPT ❋

Women were regarded as equal to men in this society in all areas except who did what jobs. Though there were many queens who had political power, there was only one female pharaoh: Hatshepsut.

3 ❋ ANCIENT GREECE ❋

Women had very few rights compared to men, and could not vote, or be elected to office, own land, inherit money, or attend public assemblies. All women were expected to marry, raise children, and manage their household.

4 ❋ ANCIENT ROME ❋

Women were not seen as equal to men — their role was managing the home and raising a family, and they could not take on public roles. Some women were able to have greater influence, such the mothers, wives, and sisters of some emperors.

⑤ ❈ MIDDLE AGES ❈

Society in the Middle Ages was controlled by the church and the aristocracy, and women were valued less than men — though they sometimes worked, they were paid less. Poetry in this time elevated women who were protected by chivalric knights.

⑥ ❈ 1700s ❈

Though women participated in the French Revolution alongside men, they were still seen as second-class citizens throughout the 1700s. They made demands for more equality, especially politically, but they ultimately did not receive it.

⑦ ❈ 1800s ❈

Gender roles were still very separated, but women started being able to more successfully make their voices heard through writing, public speaking, working, pursuing higher education, and women's rights conventions.

⑧ ❈ 1900s ❈

Women gained the right to vote in most nations (in 1920 in America). After working during the two world wars, women greatly increased their educational and job opportunities, and their traditional roles were reevaluated.

Famouse Women in History

In addition to Cleopatra and Maria Theresa of Austria, there were other women who, despite the time period they lived in, managed to make their mark on history.

❀ HYPATIA ❀
(C. 355–415 AD)

A woman of great intelligence, she was a mathematician, astronomer, and philosopher in Egypt during the Byzantine era.

BEATRICE
❀ PORTINARI ❀
(C. 1266–1290)

She inspired the great poet Dante and his character Beatrice in *The Divine Comedy*, leaving an important mark on Italian literature.

❀ ELIZABETH I
❀ OF ENGLAND ❀
(1533–1603)

At just twenty-five years old, she became queen of a country that needed to restore its reputation. Under her reign, England became a great power.

ARTEMISIA GENTILESCHI
(1593–1652/3)

She was a great painter from the Caravaggio school and was the first woman to be accepted to Florence's Academy of Design.

ELENA CORNARO PISCOPIA
(1646–1684)

She was the first woman to receive a degree from a university. (She got a degree in philosophy.) She was proficient in Greek, Latin, French, and Spanish.

JANE AUSTEN
(1775–1817)

An English novelist who is one of the most famouse women writers of all time. She wrote about ordinary people and everyday life in a time when most writers were men.

MARIE CURIE
(1867–1934)

In addition to winning two Nobel Prizes (in physics and chemistry), she discovered important information about radioactivity. She was the first woman to win a Nobel Prize.

Meanwhile, I helped Wolfgang open his trunk. "Are you nervous?" I asked.

He looked at me, and I noticed that his eyes sparkled. He answered, "No. I can't wait to play. You see, I can express myself better with notes than with words. For me, playing is natural — it's like flying is to an eagle. Music is my life."

Such wise words uttered by such a small ratlet!

Just then the royal page returned and solemnly announced, "Your Majesty would like to hear Wolfgang Amadeus Mozart!"

The time had come!

Wolfgang stuck his snout in his trunk to get his music . . . but after a moment, he shouted, "They're gone! Father, I can't find them!"

We rushed to help him. But there was no trace of his scores!

I said to Trap, "You go with Wolfgang and his family to the queen: we can't let Her Majesty wait."

Then I looked at Wolfgang and said, "I promise that I will find your scores, and I will bring them to you in time. *Mouse's honor.*"

Wolfgang nodded and gave me his paw. "Thank you, Mr. Geronimüller."

RED ALERT! HISTORY IS IN DANGER!

While Trap took Wolfgang to the royal hall, we turned his trunk **INSIDE OUT**. But there was still no sign of the scores!

I sighed and said, "Someone must have taken them . . ."

Hmm . . .

Where are they?

They aren't in here!

Benjamin nodded. "I think I know who: those two **CREEPY RATS** from the inn. They were too interested in our luggage!"

Suddenly, Trap returned. He was very happy, and burst out into a song and **dance**.

Oh yeah!   Squeak!   Woo-hoo!   Squeak!

"Calm down, everyone — no damage has been done! The hero was Trap. All of history will clap! You will say, 'Yes — he's truly a genius!' **Oh yeah!**"

Then he approached me arrogantly. "Geronimo, don't worry — I gave the **scores** to that mouseling!"

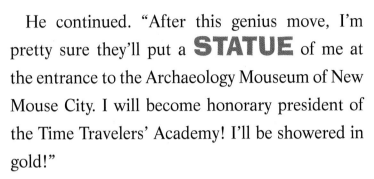

He continued. "After this genius move, I'm pretty sure they'll put a **STATUE** of me at the entrance to the Archaeology Mouseum of New Mouse City. I will become honorary president of the Time Travelers' Academy! I'll be showered in gold!"

For some reason, Trap was *not* making me feel calm. I asked, "Trap, how did you manage to find Wolfgang's scores?"

He shrugged and responded, "Easy, Geronimo: I *didn't* find Wolfgang's scores — I just gave him some random ones!"

Slimy Swiss on a stick! What was he thinking?! "What do you mean 'random'?!" I squeaked.

"You know Beaker's book? Well, I just pulled out a page, and —"

"But that's the chapter of Beethoven's* scores!" Beaker yelled, waving the book.

---

* Ludwig van Beethoven (1770–1827) was a German composer and pianist.

RED ALERT! HISTORY WAS IN DANGERRRR!

He turned to me and said, "Stilton, this is not just **any old trouble**! We need to stop Wolfgang from playing. Not only because the work isn't his, but because it was written *many years in the future*! We can't change the course of history!"

Red alert! History is in danger!

Beaker was right: there was no time to lose! I **darted** out of the room, determined to do anything to stop Mozart from playing one of Beethoven's works — before Beethoven even existed! I ran down a long corridor and finally saw an enormouse door: the *royal hall*! I burst inside, and . . .

GERONIMÜLLER, THE JESTER

The royal guards stared at me in silence. Wolfgang stared at me in silence. Marie Antoinette stared at me in silence. Basically, the entire court was staring at me in silence, until Queen Maria Theresa looked me with her fiery gaze.

"And who, may I ask, are you?" she said. "How dare you interrupt the beginning of the royal concert?"

I glanced at Wolfgang. The score was closed in front of him, so he hadn't played it yet. **HISTORY WAS SAVED!**

But I had to do something to keep it that way! So I flashed a huge smile and responded, "Who am I?! Um, I am . . . the . . . great Geronimüller, the JESTER!"

Um . . .

I took five apples . . .

The queen lifted an eyebrow. "Very well, I give you permission to perform your show before young Mozart plays."

Moldy mozzarella, now what?! How was I supposed to entertain the court and the queen?

Voilà!

I tossed them in the air like a juggler . . .

I saw a BOWL OF APPLES, grabbed five, and began to throw them above me like a juggler. But something went wrong, and all five of them bonked me on the head. Youch!

I heard whispers around the room.

"This rat is supposed to be a great jester? Humph . . . I'm not convinced!"

Ouch!

One by one, they bonked me on the head!

May I?

I asked for a lady's handkerchief . . .

There, done!

I tried to hide it behind my back . . .

Ta-da!

But when I brought out my paws, it fell to the ground!

"He's so CLUMSY!"

"If he doesn't shape up, the queen will throw him in the dungeon."

Squeak! The dungeon?! I needed another idea.

I asked a lady for a handkerchief and exclaimed, "Um . . . Geronimüller is also a magician! You see this handkerchief?"

Then I put it behind my back and tried to make it disappear. But something didn't work, and when I brought my paws out front and said, "Ta-da!" the handkerchief fell to the ground.

"This rat is supposed to be a magician?! Humph!"

"He seems a like a **cheesebrain** to me . . ."

"Maybe the queen will crush him without putting him in the dungeon first."

CHEESE NIBLETS! CRUSH ME?! WHAT COULD I DO?!

I heard a voice coming from the crowd. It was my dear nephew Benjamin! He yelled, "Uncle G, try to tell some **jokes** — they always work!"

So I cleared my throat and said, "Um, so . . . A countess called her butler — no, wait, maybe it was a *queen*. And maybe he wasn't a butler, but a page?"

Hmm . . .

I caught sight of Trap. His paw was over his eyes and he was shaking his snout. **Was I really doing so bad?!**

I looked at the queen: her eyes were two slits. Rancid ricotta! Things were definitely going **HORRIBLY**!

Her Majesty stood up and thundered, "Grab that rat and throw him in the dungeon! At once! Now! ASAP! Immediately! Move it!"

Two guards approached and lifted me up without saying a word.

I yelled, "No, wait, I think I remember the joke now . . . SQUEAK!"

As the guards were carrying me out of the room,

I heard music in the air. Cheese and crackers, it was truly *beautiful*! We were all squeakless. Even the guards put me down and stopped to listen.

I looked to the center of the room and saw Wolfgang Playing the harpsichord. But the score was closed, so it wasn't Beethoven's music. (Thank goodmouse!) It was one of Wolfgang's own compositions — he was playing it from memory! What an amazing mouse!

Empress Maria Theresa had tears in her eyes. Music truly has the power to melt your Heart and touch your soul!

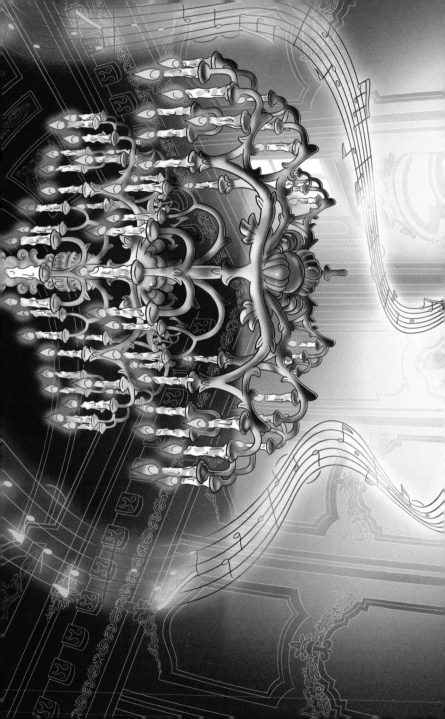

GRAB THE ARTIFACT AND LET'S JET!

Wolfgang continued to play, showing that he had quite a **prodigious memory**. Then, after a while, he did something extraordinary: the little genius turned away from the keyboard and played with his paws **BEHIND HIS BACK**! At the end of the performance, the room exploded into applause.

GREAT GORGONZOLA, WHAT AN ENORMOUSE SUCCESS!

Hee, hee, hee!

The empress was moved. She smiled, forgetting how **mad** she had been just a moment earlier.

Wolfgang got up and bowed,

happily. I could tell that, for him, playing really was the meaning of life. He saw me and walked over, carrying two scores. One was the score that Trap had ripped from Beaker's book, but the other one I didn't recognize.

"Mr. Geronimüller, I want to thank you for having tried to **HELP ME**," Wolfgang said. "Luckily, I managed to play the music from my memory, so I don't need this score! And to pay you back, I beg that you accept this new piece that I **WROTE** yesterday at the inn. It's for you!"

I took the two pieces of paper. I put Beethoven's score in my pocket (history was saved!), and then I looked at the music written by the small (but amazing!) Mozart.

I whispered to him, "Thank you from the bottom of my **HeaRt**. I will never forget you!"

At that moment, Beaker put the bananagraph under my snout and yelled, "Pesky pistachios! We only have fifteen minutes until time runs out! We need to go back!"

"Putrid Parmesan! Fifteen minutes?!"

Trap exclaimed, "Come on — grab the artifact, and let's jet!"

We all hugged the two Mozart siblings and said our good-byes.

I noticed that Trappy gave Nannerl a bracelet with a heart charm that she had with her. Trappy said, "This is for you. You're worth a lot, too, and you're a great musician. Promise me that you'll never forget your passions!"

Thank you, friend!

Nannerl hugged Trappy once more. "Thanks! I promise, my friend!"

Seeing those sweet mouselets melted my heart like fondue!

But now we needed

to run from the palace and from the 1700s: the mouseum was waiting for its **last artifact**!

Once we were safe in the palace's courtyard, we enlarged the Bananacraft. We climbed aboard, still wearing our wigs, and Beaker set the bananatimer.

THREE . . . TWO . . . ONE . . .
TAKEOFFFFFFFF!

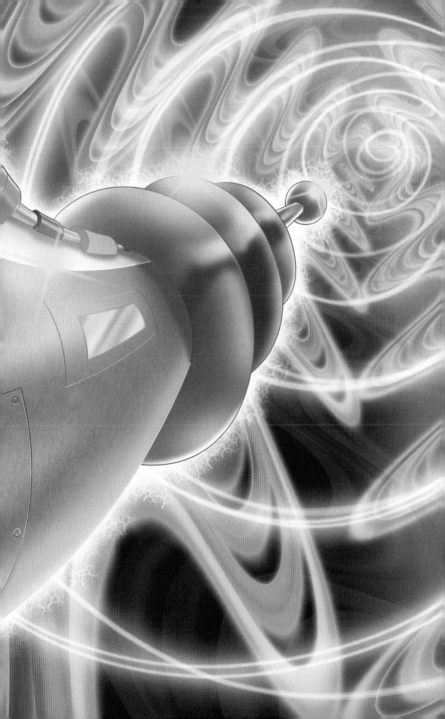

STORM!

Rat-munching rattlesnakes! Would we reach New Mouse City in time to paw over the last artifact?

While I was wondering, the Bananacraft began to move — to the **right** and to the left, up and down, faster and faster!

The lights turned off, and then turned on, and then kept turning OFF and ON again. We were tossed from one side of the Bananacraft to the other.

Squeak!

"Beaker, what is happening?!" I yelled.

Beaker tried to grab on to one of the bananaseats, and yelled, "It's a spatio-temporal storm, Stilton.

Creepellaaaa!

Let's just hope the Bananacraft follows the coordinates!"

"So there is the risk that . . . we'll get **lost** in time?" Benjamin squeaked. "Helpppp!"

Beaker nodded seriously. Then there was a crackle, the Bananacraft jolted twice, and finally an electric shock burned out all the lights inside. And suddenly, everything was calm . . . **AND DARK!**

Then the lights turned back on, and we found ourselves back at the Time Travelers' Academy. We were safe! And we were home!

Help!

It's a spatio-temporal storm!

301

We all hugged and cheered, "**Hooray!**"
The door to the Bananacraft
opened, and the three professors, Paws von
Volt, Bluster Squeak, and Cyril B. Sandsnout,
appeared.

Sandsnout exclaimed, "Quick, Geronimo,
we're still in time! *Ratmund Rattisford*
has just arrived at the mouseum and is examining
the artifacts. Did you bring the last one?"

I rummaged through my pocket and pulled out
the score that little Mozart had given me.

"Fabumouse! Let's go up to the mouseum!"

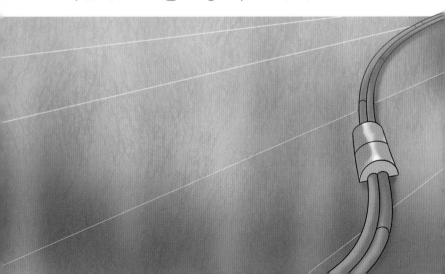

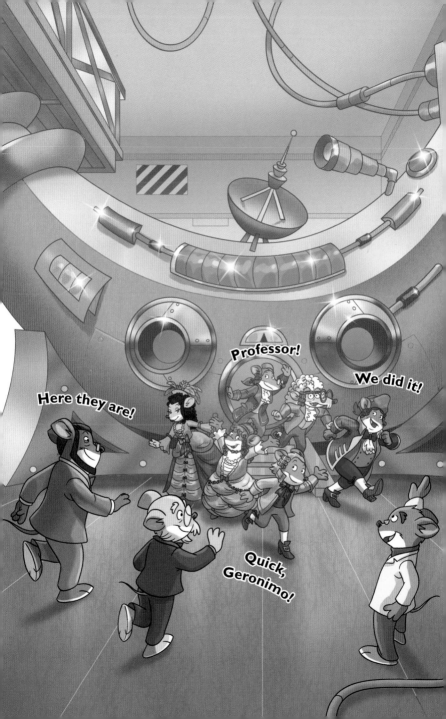

THE PRIZE IS YOURS!

We quickly went up the stairway of the secret passageway and came out on the main room of the MOUSEUM.

No one saw us as we popped out of the trapdoor.

There was a crowd of silent rodents in the mouseum's main hall, waiting as Ratmund Rattisford examined the new artifacts with a *jeweler's loupe* on his eye. He studied Alexander the Great's vase, Cleopatra's scepter (which was a surprise bonus for the mouseum!), and **Francis Drake's** gold coins.

I approached Rattisford and handed him Mozart's score. "Here, this one was missing."

He raised an eyebrow and looked at me sharply. "What a **bizarre** manner of dress you have!"

I looked down at myself — I was still dressed like

a mouse from the 1700s! I turned REDDER than a cheese rind and took my wig off.

Rattisford carefully took the SCORE I gave him and began to examine it with the loupe.

We all stood watching him, holding our breath. **Moldy mozzarella! What a tense moment!**

Ratmund Rattisford stood up suddenly, making us all JUMP in surprise. His expression went

Hmm . . . let's see . . .

from severe to bright and happy. He opened his arms and said seriously, "That to which my heart had deeply attended has come to fruition*!"

Trap huffed. "I never understand a **cheese crumb** of his speech!"

Rattisford, smiled. "Basically, what I mean is: the artifacts are ALL REAL! I am especially excited about Cleopatra's scepter: it is a true rarity, and will make this mouseum extra special and unique."

Then he took the **Petrified Cheese Prize** and pawed it to Cyril B. Sandsnout, saying, "The prize is yours, and it is most definitely well-deserved! Congratulations!"

* That means: *What I'd hoped for with all my heart has happened!*

THE TIME TRAVELERS' PARTY

Cyril B. Sandsnout organized a **big party**, which started right after we changed out of our eighteenth-century clothing. Everyone — and I mean *everyone* — came, including my sister, Thea, and even Grandfather William Shortpaws!

My grandfather put his paw on my shoulder. "You could've done better, Grandson . . ." he said. "But you really didn't do half bad!"

You didn't do half bad!

I smiled in thanks. A moment later, I felt a tug on my jacket. I turned and saw Creepella with the entire **VON CACKLEFUR** family!

Boris said, "So? How was your vacation with Creepella . . ."

"**VACATION?**"

"Yes, it sounded like loads of fun. So much adventure!"

"**Well, it was more like a mission.**"

"A mission to have a great time!"

"**No, a mission to gather artifacts for the mouseum.**"

Er . . . We had a great time!

Creepella came and **KISSED** my cheek. "We had a great time!"

Just then, Cyril B. Sandsnout asked for silence and said, "I

I want to thank Geronimo . . .

would like to THANK Geronimo Stilton for helping us find all the artifacts we needed — and an extra one, too! The **Archaeology Mouseum of New Mouse City** owes him so much!"

Everyone applauded and cheered:

"WELL DONE, GERONIMO!"

"Nice Job, Stilton!"

"Hooray!"

I blushed. "Thank you!" I said. "But actually, it isn't all thanks to me! Without MY FAMILY, and without the other time travelers, I would never have been able to do it! Thank you to Trap, Creepella, Trappy, Benjamin, Bluster Squeak, Beaker Poirat, and Paws von Volt. Each one of us helped. Together we make a really STRONG TEAM!"

I felt truly happy. We had traveled through **four different time periods** in history and managed to get back in time to save the mouseum.

And on the way, we had respected every rule of the TIME TRAVELER'S VOW!

We are strong together!

Well done!

Bravo!

A real team!

Hooray!

My dear rodent readers: don't ever forget the importance of TIME! Traveling through time has truly shown me that it can't be taken for granted.

Live every moment as if it were the most important one!

And that's the truth, or my name isn't *Geronimo Stilton*!